RUDE H[EALTH]

Born and b[   ]la
Aronson joi[   ] a
Sub-Assistan[   ]r)
and left for Australia shortly after initia-
ting the Great Tea Trolley Nastiness of
1971. She has remained there ever since.

She lives in Sydney with her husband
and two children and works as a play-
wright and screenwriter. *Rude Health* is
another brilliantly funny novel, following
in the footsteps of her first novel, *Kelp*.

What the critics said about *Kelp*:

'A charming comedy . . . its pace, wit and
sheer bizarreness are delightful.'

Guardian Education

'Full of intrigue and quite hilarious.'

Mail on Sunday

'A story which cannot help but brighten
your day. A comedy of errors which is
light-hearted, warm-hearted and genuinely funny . . . a real delight.'

The Scotsman

'A truly original and entertaining teenage
novel.'

Northern Echo

RUDE HEALTH

Linda Aronson

MACMILLAN
CHILDREN'S BOOKS

First published 1999 by Pan Macmillan Australia Pty Limited

First published in the UK 1999 by
Macmillan Children's Books
a division of Macmillan Publishers Limited
25 Eccleston Place, London SW1W 9NF
Basingstoke and Oxford
www.macmillan.com

Associated companies throughout the world

ISBN 0 330 39060 0

3 5 7 9 8 6 4

A CIP catalogue record for this book is available from
the British Library.

Printed and bound in Great Britain by
Mackays of Chatham plc, Kent

For Tony

Acknowledgements

Novels are hard to write. My solution is to shamelessly exploit the expertise and goodwill of everyone around me. Special thanks go to Nikki Christer, Cathy Proctor, Bridget Howard, Glenda Downing and all at Pan Macmillan for their patience and faith in me; to Rebecca McNally at Macmillan Children's Books, UK, for invaluable suggestions; to Mike and Michelle Aronson for inside information on the health food industry; to Gayle Burr and Rosemary Booker for advice on medical matters; to Ken Methold for advice, encouragement and pasta; and to my agent, Tony Williams, for always being at the other end of the phone. Most of all, I have to thank my long-suffering family, who take such an active part in the writing of my novels. For *Rude Health*, Jack gave wonderful plot suggestions and bits of dialogue; Lisa proofread meticulously and gave informed advice on the teenage market; and Mark, as ever, read, listened and laughed far beyond the call of duty. I owe a huge debt to you all.

Chapter 1

Mr Berkhoff gives a bloodcurdling roar. He chucks his bit of chalk at the back wall, charges from the blackboard to the front desks and bellows, 'That is enough!'

Dead silence. The bit of chalk is rolling across the floor somewhere. I'm terrified to breathe because I'm sitting in the front row with Berkhoff's enormous gut jammed up against my desk twenty centimetres from my eyes. I don't dare look upwards. He'll be frowning so hard his eyebrows will have merged into one thick black wavy line. He'll also be glaring around to see who chucked the pen top.

I close my eyes in the hope that coming to this school is some sort of nightmare and I am really back at my old school in

Sydney. I open them again. The straining belt buckle is still glinting in front of my eyes. I am still in Year 8 at Yarradindi High with Mr Berkhoff, the maths teacher from hell.

Mr Berkhoff is huge. He's tall and fat with a permanent scowl. He's sarcastic and he picks on people. He looks as if he could rip up phone directories with his bare hands. He looks as if he could rip up kids with his bare hands.

But the big thing about Berkhoff is that he's really easy to stir up. Now, I'm not a troublemaker (in fact, on balance, I'm probably a bit of a nerd) but you can understand why people target him. It was obvious to me two days ago when I first set foot in this school. You see, Berkhoff is definitely terrifying when he's furious. But he's also really funny.

Like, for example, he'll be so angry that he'll try to snap a bit of chalk. But it won't snap, and he stands there wrestling with it and making these grunting noises. Or he'll shout, 'Do you want me to walk out?' and thousands of people will shout, 'Yes!'

But the funniest thing is when he sees someone up the back mucking around. He gives this special rolling growl, yells, 'I'll teach you to play me up!' then sets off up the row at high speed.

The trouble is, because he's so fat and can't fit between the desks, he has to do this sort of sideways galloping skip with his hands held high in the air so they don't hit anything. It's hysterical. It's like a hippo doing ballet.

Of course, people up the back of the class deliberately provoke him, just to see him do it. And people in the middle of the class jam their desks closer together so he has to barge through. When this happens he lets out one of his terrible roars and smashes through like a Tyrannosaurus Rex.

One day he's going to kill someone.

But at the moment he's stuck in front of me, his huge gut still heaving. I look sideways at the Castle. The Castle is usually one desk set right out in the front of the class. It's for kids who've been mucking about. Berkhoff's class always has *two* Castle desks, and they always contain Clint Pocky and Cunningham.

'Right. Now. Let us continue.'

Berkhoff's belly moves off and the sunlight floods across my desk again. He backs towards the board, staring around, eyes narrowed. Everyone is sitting quietly. Apart from Cunningham's wheezing, you could hear a pin drop. Berkhoff picks up another piece of chalk. He takes one last piercing gaze at the class. He turns his back to finish writing up the questions.

Immediately, a hail of pen tops comes flying over my head and splatters against the blackboard. Berkhoff roars, spins round—and finds the whole class writing in their books. Apart from me. I'm frozen, staring at him.

'And what are you staring at?'

'Nothing, sir.'

'Where's your pen top?'

I look down at my ballpoint pen. It doesn't have a top. I'm aghast. I just stare at it. Then back up at him.

'You threw a pen top, didn't you?'

I am probably the only person in the class who didn't throw a pen top.

'No, sir.'

'Oh yes you did. I suppose you think it was very funny too, don't you?'

'No, sir.'

'Come out here!'

And that's when it happens. I have this habit of sitting in my desk with my feet tucked up under my bum. Today's no exception. As I jump up, I find I have pins and needles in both feet. I can't feel the ground. It's like I'm wearing thick iron boots. My legs crumple under me. I have to cling to the desk.

The whole class roars with laughter. Berkhoff makes a low, rumbling sound then bellows, 'Walk properly!'

'I can't, sir. I've got pins and needles.'

'Very amusing. You're new, aren't you? With an odd name. Ian Grubby ... Snotty ...'

The whole class rocks with laughter. Clint and Cunningham are nearly falling off their seats.

'Rude, sir. Ian Rude.' I'm still clinging to the desk, trying to drag my feet along. The pins and needles are spectacular.

'Well, Mr Rude ...' He yanks my desk, with me attached, between Clint Pocky and Cunningham. 'You can go into the Castle.'

Berkhoff slaps my chair next to my desk and my bag next to my chair. I stumble into a sitting position with the pins and needles going berserk. Clint and Cunningham give me conspiratorial grins. Twenty minutes ago, before rollcall, they were grabbing me by the shorts and giving me nonstop wedgies all around the oval. If you don't know what a wedgie is (and lucky you if you don't) it's when someone runs up behind you, yanks your trousers up so your underpants get wedged in your backside and yells, 'Wedgie-eee!' in case you hadn't noticed.

Berkhoff turns to the giggling class, bangs his hands on the desk and yells, 'Right! The next one to talk goes to the Principal.'

He turns back to the board. People start working, still muttering and giggling. Clint Pocky does an armfart. Everyone laughs. Berkhoff spins around and everything falls silent. I notice Clint Pocky grinning at me. He's doing sign language telling me to do an armfart. I turn the other way. That means I'm looking up at Cunningham's pointy head and fine black moustache. Cunningham has this big meaty laugh. Matches his big meaty gut. He looks like a pyramid. I reckon Cunningham is about twenty, just dumb.

This school is the pits. To prove the point, Andy Bogle, the class genius, starts bleeping like a microwave oven as he races through his work. What a grade-A nerd!

Don't get me wrong, I don't have anything against geniuses. But Andy is seriously weird.

For a start, he's got this strange piercing sideways look. Also, his lips keep writhing about as if they've got a life of their own. The strangest thing of all is that he keeps making these peculiar sounds all the time. He hums tunelessly. He blows raspberries. But what really spooks me is that nobody seems to notice this apart from me. Even the teacher.

Berkhoff is squeezing sideways up a row towards the back of the class. He's calmed down. He drops into his normal sarcasm. 'Now, ladies and gentlemen. If you would be so kind as to put your homework books on my desk . . .'

At least that's one thing I can do right today. I did a really good job last night. Nice neat figures. All margins done with a ruler and red pen. I've packed it in the front pocket of my schoolbag for ease of access. I plunge in my hand—to hit some kind of lukewarm sticky mess. I pull out my homework book. It's covered in fluff, bits of broken pencil leads and squashed banana.

My stomach leaps with panic. Mum

must have slipped a banana in my bag for lunch. This morning's wedgies have turned it into a pulp. I try frantically to wipe the mess off on my jumper. That just makes it fluffier. I scrape it on the desk. That just flattens it out. In complete desperation, I crouch down in my seat and start licking it.

Of course, Caroline Dillinger, class dobber, goes, 'Oh, Mr Berkhoff, Ian Rude's under the desk licking his maths homework book, Mr Berkhoff!'

The class erupts into laughter. Clint and Cunningham immediately start licking *their* books. Berkhoff, right at the back of the room, turns round snarling. Everyone looks at him in anticipation. The big question is—Is Berkhoff going to skip? There's a pause. For one fantastic moment I think I'm off the hook . . .

Then Berkhoff gives his special, rolling growl. He yells, 'I'll teach you to play me up!' And, throwing his arms in the air, he starts his angry, sideways skipping up the row.

'Mr Funny Man, eh. Mr Class Clown.'

Everyone but me is rocking in their desks with smothered laughter.

'Well let's see how funny this is.'

Someone has shoved a desk in his path. He crashes through it and bellows, 'You're on detention.'

I'm terrified. I call out, 'But Mr Berkhoff, sir . . .'

'Don't answer me back!'

'Sir, I was licking off my banana . . .'

Now a complete barrier of desks has been shoved in his way. Berkhoff throws back his head, does a Tyrannosaurus roar, smashes his way through and ends up with his hands on my desk and his face jammed right up to mine. He yells, 'You will go to the Principal!' He turns to the class. 'Shut up the lot of you.'

There's a terrible silence. He turns his face back to me. I'm petrified. His big horse's bum is high in the air. There's foam on his lips and I can see the open pores in his nose. He looks so deranged I'm scared he might bite me.

And then, my life ends. Because, at that moment, when you could hear a pin drop, Berkhoff farts. It's unmistakable. A laugh spurts out of my mouth a split second before the whole class rocks. I catch a glimpse of Cunningham laughing. He's bright red and shaking. He's like a raspberry jelly with eyes.

I gulp back the laugh and desperately whisper, 'Sorry sir, sorry sir ...'

But it's too late. Berkhoff blames *me* for the fart.

This is the most vicious teacher in the school.

And he now hates me.

Chapter 2

I'm in the Principal's room. Mr Cobbett, the Principal, is striding angrily up and down. His hands are clamped behind his back. He's tall and thin with a pointed nose, poppy eyes and an Adam's apple so big and sharp-looking you'd think it would cut him. If Berkhoff's a hippo, Cobbett is a big black crow.

I gulp.

Cobbett suddenly stops. He stares angrily at me, then yanks open a drawer in his desk. It's like in the films where the Mafia boss gets out a gun to shoot the detective. But it's not a gun that Cobbett gets out. It's a big plastic bottle of indigestion medicine and a little cone-shaped cup. He sets them right in the middle of his desk. He turns his poppy eyes on to me and waits.

What am I supposed to do? Take some? My heart is pounding. He raises an eyebrow aggressively. I'm just about to pour myself a dose when he snatches up the bottle, fills the cup to the brim and gulps it down. His Adam's apple bounces up and down like it's bungy jumping.

'Rude, I don't like smart alecs.'

He pours himself another cup of medicine.

'Mr Berkhoff has told me things about you that make me think you are a smart alec.' He gulps the medicine. 'All I can say, Rude, is that if you continue to act like a smart alec, you will sincerely regret it.' He snaps the cup down on the desk. 'I will not have you egging on Cunningham and Clint Pocky.'

Egging on Cunningham and Clint Pocky! I should get police protection from Cunningham and Clint Pocky!

'Do you hear me?'

I'm so stunned I just murmur, 'Yes, sir.'

'Have you anything to say for yourself?'

I think of telling him about the wedgies, but anyone who can seriously think I egg on Clint and Cunningham is never going to believe that.

I shake my head.

'Just a few things about this school, Rude. We are not a city school, like you are used to. We are a small country school. We are not interested in tough, streetwise behaviour. So please do not import that sort of thing into our community. Do you understand? You can go.'

I go, my heart still thumping heavily against my shirt. He's being incredibly unfair, but at least he's not threatening to tell my parents.

As I come out, I see Clint Pocky and Cunningham sitting waiting their turn with Cobbett. I don't know what exactly they're there for, but I bet it's inventive. They grin and pull faces at me like we're best friends. It's worse than them giving me wedgies.

I walk out through the school gates, furious. I don't want Clint and Cunningham to be my friends. What I want is to be back in the city, with my real house, my real school and my real friends, not these brain-dead morons. And not teachers who are so fat they need their own postcode and who fart all over the place and blame you. And I am not a person who has tough, streetwise behaviour. I am a normal human being.

The only reason I'm here is that my dad got made redundant. He was an accountant and his firm gave him a whole heap of money to go. He says it was a blessing in disguise because he and my mum have always wanted to get out of the city. He reckons it's much healthier. For him, maybe. He doesn't have to put up with the wedgies.

I should explain that my dad is the world's greatest optimist. This means he never really sees any catastrophe as a problem. Which is great most of the time. For example, if you break anything or forget something or are late or do anything that most adults would go ballistic about, Dad will never tell you off. The trouble is, when you hit what you and the rest of the world would see as a major worry, Dad just kind of ... breezes past it.

For instance, he and Mum are really busy setting up our new business but there is no way I could make him understand that when it opens I plan to die of shame. The point is, it's a health food shop and it's going to be called 'Rude Health'. I wouldn't mind that in the city. But here, people seem to think it's a huge joke—of the worst kind. Every night little groups of locals keep gathering outside the front window (where there's a sign saying: 'Rude Health Macrobiotics and Health Foods, opening shortly') and actually laughing out loud. I don't know whether they're laughing at the name or the idea of health foods or what. One thing's for sure, when the kids at school realise I'm connected with it, life is going to be even worse.

I think a lot of my problems boil down to having a name like Rude. When I was a kid I changed it. I can't believe what I changed it to. I changed my name from Rude to Cheeky. Ian Cheeky. What a dork. But Dad, you see, can't grasp that there's a problem. He says I should join in the fun. He reckons it's great being called Rude. He used to introduce himself by saying, 'My name's Rude but not obscene!' He says our next business should be a joke shop called Rude Gesture. The trouble is, he might mean it.

He's right, of course. I shouldn't let it worry me. But I do. I'm also sensitive about the fact that I'm small. But I'd be an idiot not to worry about that because it makes me such a target for thugs. Mind you, my friend Finn is really tall and he's a target for thugs as well, so you can't win.

My way home takes me down the main street. It's on the ocean. Actually, Yarradindi's pretty beautiful. If I didn't have to live here, I could quite like it.

The first thing you have to understand about Yarradindi High is that it is run by tribes. There are five tribes. The Tates, The Pockys, The Bogles, The Dillingers and The Rest. The Tates have glasses and reddish hair and tend to be weird. The Pockys are psychopaths. The Bogles are bossy and skinny (and, in the case of Andy, very strange). The Dillingers are tall, blond, muscly and even more bossy than the Bogles. And The Rest put up with it.

Except that now I'm here The Rest don't have to put up with anything since everything is taken out on me. At first I thought it was because I'm from the city. So I asked Rory Dillinger if he called me a boofhead because I came from the city. He said, 'No, it's cos you're a boofhead.'

As I glance back through the cyclone

fence that surrounds the school I see Berkhoff leaning over putting a big pile of exercise books into the back seat of his car. It's a battered red Barina Hatch. His massive butt sticks up in the air, straining against his trousers. I wish I had one of those blowpipes with poisoned darts. *Thuck*! Straight in the buttock. Meanwhile, Berkhoff gets in the car. He's so huge he practically has to bend in half. He drives off and his head's nearly touching the roof. Someone says he's coming with us to our geography camp in the mountains. Perhaps I can push him off a cliff.

And then it happens—sooner than I'd expected, but I knew it had to come. Just as I'm walking down the street, Clint Pocky and Cunningham go speeding past on Cunningham's bike. Cunningham leans out and yells, 'Yay, shortie!'

I know instantly I'm no longer his best friend. Which is fine with me. But then, and my heart sinks, he goes, 'So how's your *health food shop*?'

They shriek with laughter as they fly off into the distance.

It's started . . .

Chapter 3

I walk along the main street just to check how noticeable our shop is. It is incredibly noticeable. It's painted bright yellow. It's got the words 'Rude Health' in huge fancy letters on the window, plus a circle of leaves and a painting of a basket of fruit and grain. Actually, it looks pretty elegant, particularly in contrast to the run-down motorbike repair shop on one side and the hairdresser's on the other. Don't get me wrong. I'm glad it looks elegant. It's not that I want to be mean. I just wish it was something good like a video shop or a sports shop.

I let myself imagine about that for a moment, then let the daydream melt away. It's not a sports shop or a surf shop. It's not even an ordinary food shop.

It's a health food shop. And everyone is going to laugh.

I go in the back way.

'Mum!'

'In the front, Ian.'

Our kitchen and living room are behind the shop, but our bedrooms are upstairs. The first job was to clean it all up. That took for ever. Then it all had to be painted. Dad's still finishing painting the upstairs but the rest is done. Meanwhile, Mum's getting all the stock sorted and labelled.

As I come into the front where the shop will be, she's standing at a table. It's loaded up with a huge plastic sack of prunes, a set of scales and a heap of little plastic bags with our Rude Health logo, which is a semi-circle of leaves and the words 'Rude Health' in special lettering. She's shovelling prunes from the big sack onto the scales, then pouring them into the little bags. She's got a real rhythm going. She's little, like me and Dad.

She smiles. 'Hi. Have a good day?'

I wish I could spill out how bad it all is, but I can't. The thing is, Dad being the world's greatest optimist means that Mum does the worrying for both of them. I know she's worried that the shop won't be ready in time for our grand opening on Saturday, which is three days away. I can't make her worry about me as well. So I dump my bag and smile and say, 'Yeah, good. How was yours?'

'Oh, great. I've done all the dried fruit apart from the prunes and the apricots. Now I only have to do the nuts. I wish we didn't have to use plastic bags, but I can't find a good biodegradable alternative.'

Mum worries a lot about the planet. Especially the bit that Dad's standing on.

'Did you have your vitamins?'

'Nearly.'

I whip the bottle of pills out of my pocket. Mum—who's the health food expert of the family—has invented these new vitamin pills for teenagers which we're going to sell in the shop. They're called 'Rude Health Teenage Energy Pills' to sound a bit cooler and they've got our logo.

It wouldn't be a problem except that the day's dose is split up into five pills so you absorb them better. I feel like I'm taking pills every ten minutes. I gulp down the two that I'm supposed to have taken. Mum smiles happily. I'm hoping they'll help me get taller.

Mum puts down her scoop, reseals the big sack of prunes and wipes her hands on her apron. 'Come on, let's have a cuppa. And, Ian, you must give me that list of things you need for the school camp. Steve! Tea!'

'G'day, Ian.'

It's my dad. He's covered in blobs of cream paint.

Dad washes his hands while I fill up the kettle. Meanwhile, Mum's chattering away about the shop as she flies through the air snatching mugs and tea bags mid-flight. She has to jump for the cupboards because she's so short. We all do. I never realised how odd this looked to outsiders until Year 3, when Finn asked why my mum and dad kept bouncing around the kitchen as they did the drying up. Now I'm really conscious of it.

The hanging baskets were the worst. The one good thing about moving is that the new place has no hanging baskets. Mum used to love hanging baskets of ferns. And they did look nice. The trouble was, they were hung at just the right height for Dad and Mum, but for any other adult it was really dangerous. People were always crashing into them and getting cracked in the forehead—then in the back of the head as the stupid thing swung back.

The weirdest thing was that Mum and Dad were always surprised when people hit themselves. The point is, Mum and Dad don't think of themselves as being abnormally little. They think of everyone else as being abnormally big.

Dad dries his hands, jumps, and snatches the biscuit tin from the shelf. Suddenly there's the strangest noise from outside. It's a sort of deep, gargling roar. The back doorbell rings three times. Dad looks up from the biscuit tin.

'Oh, I forgot. That's Syd. The bloke from next door who runs the motorbike place. I invited him in.'

Mum's all anxious. 'Steve, we're opening in three days, we've got heaps to do. We don't really have time to sit and socialise . . .'

Dad smiles. 'This isn't just socialising. It's building local contacts. Syd knows everyone. He'll bring in custom.'

He opens the door. From what I can see, this is not the sort of person who's interested in health foods. It's a bald old guy in black shorts, elastic-sided boots and a torn navy blue singlet. He's beaming. He's got tattoos all over his arms. He looks like one of those happy, sweaty old men you see in beer ads ripping the tags off icy beer cans. He sticks out an oil-covered hand to Mum, gives a sort of gargled roar, nods happily in Dad's direction and shouts, 'Aaah! Seeya goya wife a betterlookin' a you, a lucky begga, aaaah!'

What? Mum and I are completely mystified.

Dad grins, pulling up a chair for him. 'Jan, Ian, this is Syd from next door.' He grins at Mum. 'He reckons you're better looking than me.'

Mum and I give forced chuckles. Encouraged, Syd sits down, beams, nods towards Dad and bawls, 'Aaah, seeya goya mor pain ona face a ona wall a silly begga, aaah!'

I'm starting to get this. He means Dad's getting more paint on his face than on the wall, and he's a silly beggar. It would be okay if he didn't shout so much. He turns to me and yells right in my ear.

'Aaah, watch a nipper a goin a school, aaah! Bag bigger'n him! Same class a young Clint a cheeky begga!'

Clint? What's he saying about Clint?

Dad's trying to protect his ears from Syd without showing it. 'Syd was saying that his grandchildren go to your school, Ian. One's in your class. Clint. Nice kid, I just met him. I've told him to come over any time he likes.'

What!

Syd grins, shakes his head proudly and yells: 'Aaah! Clint! Come a my place, chucka frisbee inna china cabinet. Smash a fifteen plates, a naughty begga, aaah!'

I close my mouth, which has dropped open with dismay. Clint Pocky coming over for social visits ... Great. Nonstop wedgies in the comfort of my own home.

Syd suddenly turns to Mum and me, frowns disapprovingly and goes into a long gargling sentence that contains the words 'camp', 'Big Tabby', 'vicious begger' and 'shotgun'.

Mum smiles brightly and says, 'Yes!' She clearly has no idea what he's talking about.

But Dad just chuckles. 'Syd reckons this school camp you're going on is dangerous, Ian. He reckons the mountains are full of savage feral cats.'

Syd gets really stirred up. 'Aaaah! Big

24

Tabby! Ripper eyes out a vicious begga, aaah!'

'He's particularly worried about a monster feral cat called the Big Tabby. He reckons you should all be issued with shotguns.'

I look at Mum. Mum looks at me. Dad's found a character. Dad loves a character. He says he spent so many years working with cardboard cutouts he's got to make up for lost time.

Syd stays for a second cup while Mum, Dad and me seal the little bags of prunes with sticky tape and stick on the 'Use by' tags. I get to use the pricing gun. Syd raves on about the Big Tabby and the dangers of the place where we're going. He makes it sound quite interesting.

When we've finished, we eat dinner and I go up to do my homework. But first I flop on my bed. I re-read the letter from my best friend, Finn, in Sydney. It makes me feel happy and homesick at the same time. I get an image of Finn. He's got a pen top stuck up each nostril. He reckons he might be able to come to stay next Easter. That'd be good.

I'm calming down. I unpack my books and say out loud, 'Ah, go to hell, Berkhoff, you fat dork.' I get quite philosophical. I can handle school. I smile and tell myself things have to get better.

What I don't know is that tomorrow I will be the kid who killed the Principal.

Chapter 4

The first thing I want to say is that it was an accident. Whatever Clint Pocky and Cunningham say, I did not go in there planning to kill the Principal. Anyway, I didn't kill the Principal and he didn't die. He had indigestion. It only looked as though he was dying. The point is, every kid in the school thought I'd deliberately killed him, and it was the beginning of my life as the evil genius of Yarradindi.

It all started because of Stretchable Nose. Stretchable Nose is a game I invented with Finn years ago when we were little kids. You pretend your nose is made of Blu Tack. Then you pretend to hook your nostril onto something like a door handle. The idea is to stretch your Blu Tack nose for as long as you can without anything touching it, so it's like this incredibly long, invisible ribbon. If anything touches it, you're out. This includes your own face, so you have to walk with your head tucked down and looking backwards over your shoulder.

Finn and I used to play it for hours. It's really hard because you have to run as fast as you can without bumping into people and you can only see out of one eye.

Now, I haven't played Stretchable Nose for years, and I admit it's way dumb. But that morning, before school, as I'm walking past the gym, I notice these two old coat hooks on the wall at eye level. They're tailor-made for Stretchable Nose. I think of Finn and chuckle to myself. I can't resist. After all, it will take my mind off wedgies and Berkhoff. I pretend to hook my nostril over one of the hooks.

Now, as I walk backwards, I pretend my nose stretches. I walk backwards a bit more. Then, I lower my head and turn my body forwards, so I'm looking over my shoulder like I'm about to do a headbutt.

I'm off! I run twice round the quad, pretending I'm racing Finn. Then I run up to the art room, back along the top corridor and down the smelly staircase near science lab one. I go out past the canteen, through the gym wing, and up the stairs. Then the first bell goes. I go faster. I have to make it down to the quad again to beat Finn and win the world record. The second bell goes. Got to make a new world record. My nose is ribboning out. I tuck my head down and fly. I go zooming past the staffroom door.

I collide with Berkhoff. My head hits him right in the stomach. I'm going so fast it's like hitting a brick wall. I reel off, clutching my head.

Berkhoff goes, 'Yuff!' and totters backwards.

He crashes straight into the Principal who's coming out of the staffroom with Mrs Mitchell. They fall down. The art teacher behind them falls down. It's like a human bowling alley. Teachers are going down like dominoes. There are screams and yells and books all over the floor. This is a nightmare. I feel as if my head has been punched down between my shoulders.

What's worse is that about twenty teachers are all getting up with furious snarls on their faces. Berkhoff's bent double, winded, glaring at me like he wants to kill me. He's got spilt tea all over him. The Principal gets to his feet. His face is so twisted with rage his forehead looks like a knot of worms.

He bellows, 'Into my office! Never, in all my born days, have I seen one boy who can make so much trouble in so short a time, I ...' Suddenly, he clutches his chest. He staggers and his poppy eyes bulge. He gasps and gives way at the knees. He croaks, 'I think it's my heart.'

Mr Thompson, the music teacher, grabs him and yells, 'Quick! Call an ambulance. He's having a heart attack.'

He's dragging Mr Cobbett to a chair. Berkhoff's trying to assist but he's still gasping for air. Cobbett's groaning out loud. His eyes roll. They settle on me. They're all mad and glassy.

He's going to die. I've murdered the Principal.

Mr Thompson dumps him onto the chair and loosens his collar and tie. Miss Nichols, the art teacher, rushes up with a glass of cold water. She holds it to Mr Cobbett's lips. He sips a bit, still staring at me with glazed eyes.

I want to say I'm sorry, but it seems the wrong moment. In the distance I hear the ambulance siren. Mrs Mitchell bundles me and some other kids off. We all look out of the window to see Mr Cobbett being wheeled out on a stretcher. It's like in the films. Already, people are starting to stare at me and whisper. A group of Year 8 girls comes up and says, 'Why did you kill Mr Cobbett?' Caroline Dillinger says, 'You'll get twenty years for murder.'

By the time we start rollcall, the whole school thinks I have murdered Cobbett and taken out Berkhoff. Clint Pocky and Cunningham are walking round behind me like bodyguards. I nervously nibble my overdue vitamin pills. On the way to music, some Year 10s come up and say, 'Are you the kid that got Cobbett?' When I say yes, they say, 'Cool!'

Just then, Mr Thompson comes in, shuts everyone up and says that Cobbett has not had a heart attack. It was a false alarm. All he had was very bad indigestion and all that is wrong with Mr Berkhoff is that he was seriously winded. Someone up the back does a disappointed 'Aaww'. Mr Thompson pretends not to hear and tells us Mrs Mitchell is going to be Acting Principal until Mr Cobbett gets back. He adds that we need to open our song books at page 10. Everyone starts talking. There's a mixture of relief and disappointment. Personally, I'm incredibly relieved.

Clint Pocky says, 'Ya should have finished 'em off.'

I'm living in dread of the fifth period maths class with Berkhoff. But he doesn't turn up. It's some old man I've never seen. We actually do some work for a change. Clint and Cunningham still think I'm worth being seen with, so they sit with me. They keep jabbing me in the ribs and showing me their scabs.

At lunchtime, instead of wedgies, I have to tell my story a hundred times. Then the rumours start. The first rumour is that Cobbett is really dead but they're keeping it from us so the Year 12s don't get upset and stuff up their exams. The second rumour is that Cobbett is not dead but has just had a real heart attack. The third rumour is that Cobbett is suing my parents for a million dollars.

That's the one that gets me. My parents haven't got a million dollars. They're sinking all their money into the shop. I get a vision of them beaming across the packing cases. I imagine Dad smiling and joking as he stands in the court room being interrogated. I feel terrible.

After school I hide in the library. When everyone's gone, I run like crazy to the newsagent's. I buy a 'Get Well' card with a smiling Alsatian's head on it. I write, 'Sorry to hear you have indigestion. From Ian Rude.' As soon as I've written it, I realise it sounds really smart-alecky. Also, maybe he will think the Alsatian is supposed to look like him. If I'm not careful he'll sue my parents for two million dollars.

I buy another card. This one has flowers on. It's really cheap-looking, but it's the only one I can afford. I don't know what to write, so I quickly scribble, 'From Ian Rude.' Just as I'm putting it in the envelope I notice it has the word 'Con-gratulations' written in white letters under the flowers. Terrific. 'Congratulations on having a heart attack.' I can't believe I'm so stupid. Now I'm broke—on top of everything else.

I rip up both cards and chuck them in the litter bin. As I turn away I'm face to face with a huge gut. It's unmistakable. I gulp. I look upwards.

Berkhoff looks down at me, narrows his eyes and says, 'Some people think what happened was an accident, Rude. Well . . .' He lowers his huge vicious head menacingly. 'I don't!'

I feel a shiver go down my spine. That man is evil. He glowers at me some more, then strides off. I feel like chucking something at him, but I'm too scared. Anyway, it would probably bounce off.

I go to the beach. It's soothing. The sea crashes in and sucks back. A big seagull walks along the beach. Its big poppy eyes remind me of Cobbett. I sigh. Well, at least he's not dead. Cobbett that is, not the seagull. I wish Berkhoff was dead. No. I wish Berkhoff was going through terrible agonies somewhere, that's what I wish. What I wish most is that I was back in the city.

When I get home, there's a refrigerated truck parked outside our back gate. It is delivering great big cardboard cartons. Mum's getting one out of the back. She looks up anxiously and yells, 'Ian, can you help? The vegeburgers have arrived.' Dad's halfway up the path towards our new storeroom staggering under two boxes. He's beaming. He says, 'Grab a box, Ian. Looks like we're in business.'

Mum and Dad have arranged for a health food manufacturer to make this burger thing out of carrots and other vegetarian stuff. They sent us a photo. It comes in an air-tight plastic wrapper with our special Rude Health logo. It is flat and round. It is a sort of dark brown with orange and green flecks. It looks gross. It's exactly like every other vegeburger except that it contains extra vitamin B_{12} which, according to Mum, is the vitamin most vegetarians miss out on. Dad plans to sell nationwide. He reckons we'll make a fortune with the right advertising.

Plunky, happy music. A grinning family is sitting around the dinner table. The mum appears with a huge dish of Rude Health vegeburgers. The kids' eyes light up. They are thrilled. Who needs McDonald's? They can't wait to get their teeth into that extra vitamin B_{12}. The dad sniffs his plate in ecstasy. The teenager and the ten-year-old grin at the mum. The cute little toddler beams into the camera. She lisps, 'Oo, yummy.' And throws up.

Dad walks past carrying his carton of vegeburgers. He's smiling absently. I think at this moment he's daydreaming something like him, Mum and me making millions from a chain of fast-food restaurants selling the vegeburger. They will be just like McDonald's. They will be called McRude's and you will be able to buy a Big Rude, French Fries and a Coke on special.

Suddenly I hear a sound that makes my blood run cold. There is a high-pitched giggle. I stop in my tracks. Clint Pocky? It can't be! Then I hear a cheerful bellowing gargle.

'Aah put 'em 'ere a Clinta liddle-begga!'

Dad comes out of the storeroom grinning.

He says, 'Guess what, Ian, we're going to a barbecue next door. And all the grandchildren will be there!'

Chapter 5

My heart seizes. Clint's bound to tell my parents about Cobbett and Berkhoff.

Dad dumps a carton into my arms. 'Here you go. Our contribution to the barbie. Take them to Syd's . . .'

He's not serious? Taking vegeburgers to a Pocky barbecue? This is instant humiliation.

'But Dad . . . these are vegeburgers!'

'That's right. We're test-driving them on the Pockys. If we can get the Pockys interested, we'll get the whole town interested. Look . . .'

He lowers his voice and glances around to check Syd and Clint can't hear. Since Syd is now roaring cheerfully off down the path with Clint giggling happily in a headlock, it's a safe bet.

Dad's face is close to mine.

'I know they're a bit rough and ready, Ian, but people like the Pockys—they're the salt of the earth.'

I stare at him.

'It's true. In a crisis—say your house catches fire—you can bet your bottom dollar it'll be blokes like the Pockys who'll drag you out.'

I'm about to say you can bet your bottom dollar it'll be blokes like the Pockys who set it alight in the first place, but I don't. I recognise that his mind's made up. I drag a smile across my face and shift the box into a more comfortable position. Perhaps, with the vegeburger to talk about, the Pockys won't tell my parents about Cobbett.

As I stagger in through the back gate to the Pockys' backyard there's an almighty 'Whoomph'. It's Syd, chucking a can of kerosene onto the barbecue. Flames shoot up in the air. A big cheer goes up from an army of little Pockys swinging around and around on the rotary clothes hoist. Syd waves to them and gargles a greeting at me. I'm about to call back when I get a rabbit punch between the shoulder blades and drop the box. I turn around to see salt-of-the-earth Clint. He lets out a high-pitched giggle.

There's a slightly deeper version of the giggle from a man walking up to us. He's got to be Clint's dad. He's got waist-length blond hair, pointy features, black shorts and a black singlet that reads: DON'T BE A YOB, GIVE POCKY THE JOB. He's got half a tree balanced on one shoulder and a chainsaw slung over the other. Like Clint, he's grinning.

'So this is the kid who put Cobbett in hospital.' He turns to Syd, nearly wiping me out with the tree, and bellows, 'Eh, Dad. This is the kid who put Cobbett in hospital.'

From the barbecue, Syd lets out a roar and waves his kero tin. How can I shut them up? I look nervously around for my parents. Clint's dad chucks the log on the lawn. The ground shakes.

'I'm Terry. Good on ya for getting Cobbett, mate.' He wrenches at the starter cord of the chainsaw. 'Rotten old mongrel. He called my kids roughnecks . . .'

There's a thunder of corrugated iron and screaming as three miniature Pockys go running across the roof of our shed chucking lemons.

The chainsaw roars into life. Clint's dad starts ripping into the log. 'What I said to him was ...' he's screaming at the top of his voice, 'if you can't discipline them ...' the sawdust is flying out in a long stream, 'ya shouldn't be in the job. If ya can't stomach the mustard ...' he switches off the chainsaw, 'then don't offer your sav.'

He suddenly throws down his chainsaw, drops into a tae kwon do position and shouts, 'Kee-aaaa!'

Clint does the same.

In a flash, they're throwing kicks and doing oriental whoops all around the yard. A gang of little Pockys joins in on Clint's side. Terry Pocky's being kicked and chopped and punched from every side, but he's laughing his head off. So are all the little Pockys. Syd's cheering. It's insane.

I'm just wondering whether I could sneak off home when I see my mum and dad entering with bowls of dessert and salad. They're a bit taken aback by the ball of walloping Pockys, but Syd roars and waves and beckons them in. Terry Pocky beams, snatches up the chainsaw and comes striding towards Mum and

Dad. One kid's still hanging round his throat but he doesn't seem to notice. I can't let him tell them about Cobbett. I desperately try to think of a distraction.

I burst out, 'Look at the chainsaw, Dad!'

Terry's grin widens. He turns on the chainsaw, holds it up in the air and revs it a few times.

'Little bewdy, eh!'

'Watch out for the little boy.' My mum's all white.

'He'll be right. We haven't lost one yet, have we, mate.' He grins at the kid. 'This is Troy. What do we say to strangers, Troy?'

There's a moment where my parents beam encouragement, then Troy lisps, 'Nick off.'

Pocky's dad cracks up. 'Ha! D'you hear that! Cheeky beggar! Naughty boy, Troy. That's very naughty!' He sticks out his hand. 'Terry Pocky. Martial Arts and Home Maintenance. Dad tells me you're in the health food business. What I wanna know is, what d'ya feed this bloke?'

He's pointing at me. My stomach does a somersault. The Cobbett story's about to come out! But Mum interrupts, beaming.

'Well, personally, I think it's all down

to vitamins and a sensible diet. I've got Ian on Rude Health Teenage Energy Pills, with odourless garlic, five times a day. And, of course, green vegetables.'

Terry Pocky's blond face clouds with bewilderment. I'm out of here. I mutter an excuse about putting the dessert we brought into the fridge, and head off with it towards the back door of Syd's house. I suppose the business about Cobbett will come out sooner or later. I just don't want to be around when it does. Particularly since the Pockys are bound to tell it like I'm some kind of serial killer.

I whip into Syd's house through the back door. I'm in a hallway between the kitchen and the living room. On the wall there's a big stuffed wild pig's head. It's snarling and there's a cigar stuck between its fangs. There's a baseball cap hanging from one tusk. Dangling from the other there's a little red lacy heart-shaped satin cushion saying: WORLD'S BEST GRANNY.

No one's here. It occurs to me that I could just dump the bowl of dessert somewhere and slip off home. They wouldn't miss me for a while and, by the time they did, the barbecue might be over. One thing's for sure. I'm going to die of embarrassment when the first vegeburger hits the griddle.

Then I notice something. In the corner of the kitchen there's a skinny young guy in shorts and a singlet standing with his back to me at a table. The table is covered with oily spare parts from some kind of engine, and the young guy is busy with a spanner. You can see all the sinews on his scrawny legs. His arms are so long and thin and brown he looks like a stick insect.

If he sees me I'll have to stay. I carefully lower the dessert bowl onto a sideboard so it doesn't make a clunk. I start to tiptoe out. Suddenly there's this savage barking. A fat old cattle dog's hurtling up the hall towards me. The young guy spins round—and it's an old lady! I nearly die of shock. My heart's pounding. It's a kid's body except with an old lady's wrinkly face and these weird little boobs. It's like a horror movie.

'Oh, shut up, Ripper.'

Ripper's snarling at me, baring his teeth. He's got a big black collar covered in metal studs. The old lady grabs him by the collar and hauls him off up the hall. She opens the door, shoves him out and shouts, 'Outside, you boofhead.'

She strides back up the hall and folds her oil-covered arms. I notice that between her boobs there's a tattoo of a crocodile with its jaws open.

She smiles. 'G'day. I'm Clint's granny. You must be Ian who got the Principal.'

Clint's granny explains that she's just fixing a fiddly bit of a vintage motorbike and won't be a minute. She says motor-bikes are all individuals and this one is a cow. She tells me to put the dessert in the fridge, then take a huge pile of plates outside. There are enough for an army. And sure enough, just as I stagger out with them, about fifty Pockys come burst-ing in through the back gates. They're all skinny, blond and manic. Meanwhile, my dad's chatting with Terry Pocky while Mum's at the barbecue with Syd. She's holding Troy.

Syd sees me, grins and stabs the air with his barbecue fork. 'Aaah! Gorra plates, a starving, a liddel beggas!'

As I dump the plates on the table next to Syd, I notice, with relief, that there are only sausages and steak on the barbecue. Then Mum calls out, 'Ian, I've got to hold the baby. Will you get out the vege-burgers?'

I freeze. I can't do this, I'll be a laughing stock. But there's no way out because Terry Pocky and Dad are coming over followed by Clint and an army of Pocky kids.

'Come on, Ian, help your mother.' It's Dad.

'Clint, Dylan, give him a hand,' says Terry.

Before I know what's happening, the Pocky kids run screaming at the box and start ripping it open. They're chucking plastic vegeburger packets at Syd, who tries to spear them in mid-air with his fork. There are packets flying about like frisbees. Ripper grabs a packet and runs off with it. My dad's laughing and trying to catch him. My mum goes into the advertising blurb.

'This is the double carrot and pea flavour. They're made of a mixture of soy beans, carrots, peas, potatoes and mushrooms. They contain added vitamin B_{12} which is often lacking in vegetarian diets. You'll be able to buy them at the shop from the day after tomorrow.'

By now, the entire Pocky clan is gathered, watching and pointing. Clint's big brother Dylan bashes his head against a tree.

'And for those of you interested in recycling, the containers are one hundred per cent recycled plastic.'

I think the Pockys' idea of recycling would be to share each other's chewing gum, but they nod and chatter as if they're really impressed. Syd holds up his hand for silence. 'Aaah! Wanna bidda hush, a noisy beggas! Here . . .'

He opens a packet, stabs a pile of vegeburgers with his fork and flicks them onto the barbecue. The barbecue lets out a huge sizzle, the Pockys press forward to watch. I've never seen vegeburgers cooking. They look like discs of compressed sick. There's a stunned silence. I'm amazed at how polite the Pockys are being. Then Terry lets out a big snort of a laugh. 'Struth! They look like something that sticks to your shoe!'

A big roar of laughter goes up.

My mum's grinning bravely. 'At least some innocent animal didn't die to give us our dinner.'

'No, it puked.'

The Pockys roar. Syd lets out a big gargle of disapproval.

'Aaah! Dunno wha' you're on abou' a silly begga! I'll have a vegeburger, lovely gruba lucky beggas!'

The laughter dies down. Syd throws a disapproving look at Terry and flicks the vegeburger onto a plate. Apart from the sizzling there is now complete silence. Troy Pocky yells 'Nick off!' but no one seems to notice because Granny Pocky has come to the front of the crowd right next to me.

'So will I, Syd!'

The oil has gone from her hands and she's got her arms folded menacingly. She's frowning. The crocodile down her cleavage is all scrunched up so its eye bulges and the rest is lost in leathery wrinkles. That's the cue. Terry Pocky's face splits into a smile.

'And me! Gimme two!'

Now all the Pocky adults start asking for vegeburgers. Relief washes over me. With the vegeburger to talk about, nobody's going to be thinking of Cobbett. At last I can relax.

My parents are both beaming and smiling so much that I decide to jump in the deep end and tell them about Cobbett. I gulp, turn to Dad and say casually, 'You know our Principal, Mr Cobbett?'

'Oh yeah. He's sick, isn't he?' Dad's still smiling and casual. He suddenly chuckles and leans over to me. 'Hey, you know what Terry Pocky told us? Told us some mad story about you headbutting some teacher and landing the Principal in hospital. Isn't that priceless? And how some nurse said he's going to sue us for a million dollars' damages. See, Ian, that's what I love about living in the country. Wall-to-wall characters. You never know what they'll come up with next.'

He chuckles. I chuckle—in fact, I burst out into big barks of nervous laughter and have to pinch myself hard on the inside of the elbow to shut myself up. Cobbett wouldn't sue us. Or would he?

Chapter 6

The next morning at breakfast Dad is assuring Mum we'll be ready for the shop to open tomorrow, as planned. Mum is not at all convinced and is getting very heated with him. It turns out that Dad's cancelled the handyman Mum had arranged to install the rest of our shelving this morning, and got Terry Pocky to come and do it tonight. Mum's convinced Terry won't do it on time, particularly since he's supposed to be babysitting Troy at the same time.

Dad simply can't see the problem. They're both pretty tense. They'd be even tenser if they knew that Cobbett might actually sue them.

I'm just walking to school planning what I'd say in court, when an angry cow moos deafeningly in my ear.

It's not a cow. It's the novelty hooter on Terry Pocky's four-seater ute. I know it's Terry Pocky's ute because on the side of it is written POCKY FENCING AND HOME MAINTENANCE and DON'T BE A LOUSE, LET POCKY FIX YOUR HOUSE. Also, Troy is sitting in the tray next to the dog, which is barking savagely and nearly strangling itself on its leash trying to get me.

Terry Pocky is in the driving seat. Three little Pockys are fighting on the front seat and Clint and Dylan are fighting in the back. Thrash music is belting out of the radio. This is actually quite good because it means that a bunch of old ladies in the bus shelter can't hear that Troy is armfarting at them.

Terry leans over and opens the front door. 'Carn, Ian! Hop in! Don't mind old Ripperson. He won't bite. Anyhow, knowing you, if he did, you'd bite him back.'

He lets out a high-pitched giggle. I can see he won't take no for an answer. I can also see he thinks I'm a total hero. I duck past Ripperson's bulging eyes and strangled demented barking and squeeze myself next to the little Pockys. They all grin and punch me in welcome. Terry revs the engine and giggles. 'So. Who you gonna deck today?' We roar off at eighty k's an hour. I grab the door handle and hang on for dear life.

Terry drives like a complete maniac. He's talking to me as we go. I think it's about building fences, but it's hard to hear over the music. Also, every time we overtake, he leans on the horn. It sounds as if a heavy metal band is chasing a demented cow down the freeway. The little Pockys next to me keep up the punching to show how much I mean to them. One of them explains that Ripperson got his name through being son of Ripper.

Meanwhile, in the back, Clint and Dylan are having an arm-wrestling competition and making suggestions as to how I should finish off Berkhoff. A motorist calls Terry a bloody idiot. All the Pocky kids cheer.

When we get out of the ute, I duck away from Ripperson's fangs to find I'm being mobbed by a huge gang of the toughest kids from the entire school.

'Eh, Rude, what ya gonna do to Berkhoff today?'

Cunningham says, 'He's gonna punch him in the head. Aren't you, Rude!'

'Yeah! Rude's gonna take out Berkhoff.'

Suddenly they're all saying it. I'm going, 'No! No, I'm not!' but nobody's listening.

Then a hush falls. From out of the crowd slouch three towering Year 12s with wild hair, terrible acne and half-closed eyes. I've seen them before. In fact, the lady in the post office pointed them out to me and Mum the day after we got here. She said to make sure we locked the car. She called them the Ratbag Criminal Element. They stare down at me. Then the one in the middle puts his hands in his pockets and drawls out of the side of his mouth, 'Hey, shortarse. Hear you got chucked out of your last school for bashing the music teacher and smashing up a grand piano.'

Everyone gasps, including me.

A kid says, 'How do you smash up a grand piano?'

Another kid says, 'Dunno. With a hammer?'

I yell, 'I did not smash up a grand piano with a hammer.'

Someone shouts, 'He did it with an axe.'

A girl screams. People start going 'An axe! An axe!' The younger kids back away like I'm going to murder them. But the Ratbag Criminal Element just exchange looks. The middle one steps forward. He stares down through narrowed eyes and whispers, 'Headbutt me, why don't cha . . .?'

Just as I'm about to faint, people start going, 'Teacher! Teacher!' Someone is coming through from the back of the crowd. I have a sudden moment of panic thinking it might be Berkhoff—who's just dying to find a reason to bust me. But it's not Berkhoff. It's a woman. In fact, it's a worried-looking sports teacher with glasses and a big nose.

She frowns, sucks air through her teeth, and says, 'All right, everyone, move along, the bell's about to go.'

Realising murder is not going to happen, everyone has drifted off. She turns to me, frowning anxiously.

'You okay?'

I nod.

'Are you sure?'

I nod again.

She's still staring anxiously at me. She suddenly sucks air between her teeth and says, 'My name's Ms Pewty, that's "Ms" not "Miss", and I'm here for a few weeks. I have a particular interest in bullying.' And she strides off. Great. She should meet Berkhoff. They could bully people together.

I hurry off, sticking close to the wall for safety. This is crazy. Now I'm a mad axeman and the Ratbag Criminal Element feels duty bound to take me out. During rollcall various people are whispering and pointing at me. It suddenly occurs to me that this morning there were no wedgies.

That has to be a plus. Maybe I should pretend I *am* a mad axeman. At least that would keep the lower school at bay. On the way to get changed for sport, I go via the deserted quad to avoid the others. Scurrying along, I catch a glimpse of myself reflected in a window. I bare my teeth. Not bad. I add a frown and half close my eyes. I look like a vampire. I check what I look like sideways. I growl softly. Out of the corner of my twisted-up eye I suddenly see Berkhoff glaring at me. His eyes narrow. He totally hates me.

He growls, 'Okay, Rude, I've got you for sport. And I warn you, one false move...'

He doesn't finish his sentence because, from far across the deserted quad, comes a loud echoing raspberry. Berkhoff spins round. The quad is completely empty. He turns back to me. He's willing me to be smiling so he can punish me. I'm not smiling. In fact, I'm terrified.

'Did you hear anything, Rude?'

'No, sir.'

'Are you sure?'

He stares at me. 'Good. Get changed quickly. Or else.'

The oval is milling with people. Berkhoff blows a whistle and tries to sort us into teams. He's still in his ordinary clothes. He doesn't usually take us for sport. Everything is disorganised because of Cobbett being away and Mrs Mitchell having to take his place. Berkhoff has to take the boys from one Year 8 class and one Year 9 class together. Ms Pewty, the worried-looking substitute teacher who rescued me, has got the girls. She takes them off to the netball courts. Meanwhile, Berkhoff is irritably picking teams for footy. He's ratty because he just stood in a mud patch and sank up to his ankle.

During selection I try to look vicious to deter people from thumping me in the game. I'm doing pretty well, really. In fact, very well. This isn't so bad. I practise sneering at a passing Year 7. I wrinkle my lip at a guy in Year 8.

Berkhoff bellows, 'Ian Rude, over here.'

I get to my place to find myself opposite a Year 9 who is a metre taller than me.

He looks down and says, 'Think you're tough, eh?'

Meanwhile, Berkhoff's at the centre ready to start the game. He keeps looking irritably at his mud-covered foot.

He shouts out, 'Right. I want a clean game. No fighting.'

He blows the whistle. The game starts. Berkhoff turns his back. *Thump*. About ten kids jump me. Up close, grass has a smell like lettuce, and sports shirts smell like ironing. Berkhoff blasts on the whistle and starts yelling. The kids climb off me. Cunningham takes the kick. As soon as Berkhoff turns his back, the kids jump me again. *Thump*. Lettuce, sweat and ironing. Berkhoff blows the whistle and bellows.

Pocky takes the kick then turns round and thumps me. So I kick him. Cunningham goes to kick me, and someone trips him. A huge ball of people is suddenly rolling all round the pitch—with me at the bottom. Heaven knows where Berkhoff's gone. Everyone is yelling. Someone's knee is pressed into the mud next to my eye. Someone's calf muscle and rolled-down sock get jammed up against my face. I can't breathe!

Then something snaps inside my head. With a big surge of fury, I sink my teeth into the calf and hang on. There's this bloodcurdling yell. I don't care, I'm triumphant. Why didn't I think of this before? I bite harder. It tastes like musty ham. The knot of bodies rolls. Someone's shrieking. I get kicked in the back. My nose is bleeding, but I hang on. Blue sky! I'm drooling and my jaw is aching but I won't let go. Through a hole in the knot of bodies I see Berkhoff across at the netball courts talking to Ms Pewty, the substitute.

Suddenly everyone's going, 'Berkhoff's coming! Quick, Berkhoff!' and struggling to their feet. I let the leg go. My mouth is all dry and leg tasting. The calf muscle belongs to some Year 9 I've never seen in my life. He's staring at me in sheer terror.

He says, 'He bit me on the leg.'

What have I done? I'm turning feral like the rest of them! What's worse, Berkhoff's going to blame me for starting it. Everyone's trying to get the game going again so Berkhoff won't know anything's happened. I stagger to my feet. I mustn't let him see the guy's leg. But where *is* Berkhoff? He's completely disappeared! People are shouting, 'The ball! The ball!' I glance sideways and see the ball hurtling towards me. Totally panicked, I kick wildly.

I'm expecting the ball to flop pathetically a metre away. But it's a brilliant kick. The ball flies off in a huge, graceful curve. Everyone goes, 'Aaaah!' It's going for ever. It arches right off the field and turns smoothly around towards the library building. People start congratulating me. This is cool.

Then, like in a bad dream, Berkhoff, irritably dragging a net of footballs, suddenly appears from behind the library building, right in the path of the ball! Everyone gasps. In slow motion the ball falls right towards him. Berkhoff shambles on.

Smack!

Right on his head.

Chapter 7

He drops like a stone. Now I've killed Berkhoff. Except that he gets up, swearing and doing his Tyrannosaurus roar and clutching his head.

My mouth is hanging open with amazement. I'm shaking with terror. Why is this happening to me? I suddenly notice everyone looking at me. But it's not just that they're looking. It's *how* they're looking. With awe. I can hear the whispers. 'Rude got Berkhoff in the head!' 'Rude took out Berkhoff!' 'Told you he'd get him in the head!'

Berkhoff yells, 'Who did that?'

There's total silence until an unmistakable female voice echoes out from the netball court, 'Oh, Mr Berkhoff, it was Ian Rude, Mr Berkhoff.'

'Ian Rude!'

It's not a shout. It's a roll of thunder. Berkhoff comes staggering towards me clutching his head. Everyone peels back to let him through. As he comes closer I see his face is smeared with mud and one eye is bloodshot and half closed like he's just been in a boxing match.

He stands staring at me, too angry to speak. Then he roars, 'You did that on purpose!'

'No, sir!'

'You kicked a ball into my head!'

'It was a fluke sir! Just a lucky kick . . .'

What am I saying—a lucky kick . . .

'A lucky kick!'

'I mean, an accident!'

'I'll give you "accident". I'll teach you to play me up.'

'Is everything all right? I heard there's been an accident?'

It's Ms Pewty, the worried substitute teacher, powering up from the netball courts.

'Not an accident, Ms Pewty. An assault. A football has been kicked into my head as I came out from behind the library buildings. By this extremely clever young man here, Mr Ian Rude. Come on Rude, move.'

He's herding me off towards the school buildings. Ms Pewty follows.

'That's terrible. Did you lose consciousness? I am a trained paramedic, you know. I can help.'

'Thank you, Ms Pewty. Luckily I did not lose consciousness. But the ball came at sufficient force to knock me out. It came from way back there—way back behind the line there.'

Ms Pewty makes a little snort of surprise and stops in her tracks.

'This boy aimed a ball from all the way back there to hit you as you came out from behind the library ... But that demonstrates *fantastic* ball control.'

Berkhoff's eyebrows shoot up. He's about to be sarcastic but he realises we're all watching.

He growls, 'I dare say.'

Ms Pewty says hurriedly, 'I mean, it's dreadful if he did aim at you, but that kick would be hard for a professional player, let alone a boy of this age.'

She turns to me.

'Ian. Did you aim that ball?'

'No. No, honestly. It was a fluke. I'm lousy at footy.'

We're stopped. Ms Pewty turns to Berkhoff. There's a pause.

Berkhoff can't restrain himself. He says, 'Please say if you feel I'm being too severe, Ms Pewty. I've only been smacked in the temple with a blunt object. I might be concussed.'

To my amazement, Ms Pewty says exactly the opposite of what Berkhoff intended. She says seriously, 'I am a little worried about that. And I would definitely like to get some ice on that eye, that's looking serious. Ian, could you wait over there, please.'

She takes Berkhoff aside and starts talking to him and checking out his eye. Meanwhile, Berkhoff's checking *her* out, frowning. I reckon he's enjoying the attention. When you're as ugly and horrible as he is you probably don't get much attention. I can't imagine you'd get any women interested in you.

Berkhoff and a woman. What a gross thought.

I stand there waiting. I glance back towards the others. They're all staring fascinated, waiting for something to happen. Just then Berkhoff comes over. His eye looks terrible. It's so swollen you can't even see the eyeball. I'm expecting to be put on detention for life, but he just says, 'I have to go and get this eye seen to. I'll deal with you later. Go back to the game.'

I just stare at him. His good eye rolls angrily.

'Well, go on!'

I'm off like a shot. My mind is spinning. Why is this happening? It's like I'm jinxed. As I come back to the others I'm mobbed. People keep asking me why Berkhoff let me off. Others want to know if I was actually aiming for his head or just his body generally. The word goes around that Berkhoff is scared of me. Clint Pocky tells me he's taking bets on a fight between me and some Year 9 who wants to take me to the wood technics room and put my head in a vice. I tell him I'm not going to fight. Clint says that's okay. If I don't turn up, he and Cunningham will just take the money and go to McDonald's.

In the changing room everyone's whispering and pointing. I suddenly remember the vitamins and take one. Andy Bogle is tying his shoelaces. He looks up, writhes his lips about and says, 'If it comes to an assault charge, you've got a good case.'

When I walk in to maths, a cheer goes up. Berkhoff hasn't arrived and there's a fever of anticipation. The only one not interested is Andy Bogle. The rest of the class crowds around me, asking whether this time I'll go for a knockout.

Then, someone shouts that Berkhoff's coming. Everyone rushes to their desk and there's a sudden hush. I gulp down a vitamin pill and try to think of something else. Berkhoff strides in, slaps his books on the front desk, and glares about. His black eye is now purple and so puffed up it's completely closed. It's gross. Everyone looks at me. Berkhoff frowns, coughs, deliberately *doesn't* look at me and starts talking about algebra.

You can tell he's rattled. So am I. I'm hardly daring to breathe.

Now Berkhoff makes us work on our own. His good eye keeps flicking about. As he strolls down the rows, people are turning in their chairs behind his back and whispering encouragement to me. Clint makes knifing signs. Cunningham's signalling that I should cut Berkhoff's throat. I'm totally stressed.

Berkhoff's getting closer. I gulp down another pill.

He's getting closer! Now he's next to me!

I look up. His good eye looks down. I drop my pen.

We both go, 'Aaah!'

As soon as the bell goes for lunch I'm out of the room. At least nothing happened to him.

Then I hear he fell over on the way to the staffroom and cut his hand.

I really am jinxed. And the terrible thing is, every time something more happens with Berkhoff, the Ratbag Criminal Element have more reason to beat me up.

I see them slouching menacingly across the quad. I strike up a conversation with the woodwork teacher by asking what is his favourite wood. He gets all fired up. He talks about lathes and books called things like *Know Your Joints* and *A Manual of Wood Turning*. Meanwhile the Ratbags are lurking. I launch into my views on chisels, and ask him his. I'm there so long I have to pretend I want to start up my own woodwork club. I've nearly got to the point of promising to make a chest of drawers when the bell rings.

At last, school is over. I plan to miss the fight with the feral Year 9 by hiding until four o'clock. I notice the games shed door is open. Excellent! I dart inside. It's dark and damp smelling. It's full of footballs and baseball bats and junk. I duck around behind a partition and dump my bag. Finally, I can relax.

I'm just daydreaming about being back at my old school when I hear someone coming. I squat down and sneak a look through a crack. It's Ms Pewty. She's got a clipboard. She's frowning and tutting to herself as she checks the equipment. She keeps writing things down.

Something is digging into my back and my leg aches from crouching. I'm trying to breathe really quietly. The thing stuck in my back is killing me, but I daren't move. I shift slightly. It's still digging into me. I shift again. And an avalanche of balls and cricket stumps comes raining down on top of me.

Chapter 8

There's an agonising moment of silence. Then Ms Pewty frowns, sucks air between her teeth anxiously and says, 'Ian, I've really been trying not to notice you, but I think it's time for you to come out now.'

I come out, dying of embarrassment. She's staring at me with that same worried look. I wish she wouldn't. It makes me feel even more anxious than I already am.

She says, 'Look, it's none of my business why you're hiding, but if you're in trouble, you can tell me.'

I think about it. It's a kind thought, but she's looking so worried already, she'd probably have a nervous breakdown if I told her. And I'd probably be beaten to death by the Ratbag Criminal Element.

So I say, 'It's okay, Ms Pewty.'

But she's still looking at me through her thick glasses in that concerned way. She sighs and sucks air in through her teeth. She's very kind. She also has amazing boobs, but I pretend not to notice so as not to appear sexist.

'Look, Ian, I know it's not really my business, but I wonder if I could have a word. The thing is, Mr Berkhoff says you keep, well, *attacking* him.'

'I don't mean to. He just keeps walking into things . . .'

'Don't get upset. I'm only trying to help. Now listen to me. Ian, have you heard of the subconscious mind?'

'What, like your sort of . . . secret mind that you're not in control of?'

'Exactly. You see, it's quite possible for your subconscious mind to make you do things that you secretly want to do but would be too scared to do openly. For example, you might not want to go to the dentist, so you might quite genuinely forget the time of your appointment and miss it. You know what I think? I think you secretly want to hurt Mr Berkhoff, and so you do.'

I'm about to say that most of the school secretly wants to hurt Mr Berkhoff, but I just shrug. Perhaps she's right. Perhaps it is all a matter of my subconscious mind. It's a more comforting explanation than being jinxed, and certainly more sensible.

Ms Pewty says, 'May I give you a hint on how to cope with your angry feelings towards Mr Berkhoff? It's something a sports counsellor once told me.'

I don't normally have much time for counsellors. There was one at my old school. I never went to see him, but apparently he shouted because he was deaf and he had such terrible bad breath that kids nearly passed out the minute they walked into his office. People would go in and he'd lean across the desk, stick out his hand, shout 'Hi'—and nearly burn the paint off the wall behind them.

Still, this person could be different. Anyhow, I need all the help I can get. I nod.

'Well, it's this. If you feel your levels of aggression or anxiety rising, you channel them into your upper body. Then, keeping your fists clenched, you flex and unflex your arms—until your stress works itself completely away. Watch.'

She puts down her clipboard, frowns,

sucks air between her teeth and sticks her arms out like a little kid playing aeroplanes—but completely serious. Then, she starts bending her arms in and out at the elbow, like a muscleman.

'You see? This way you get rid of your aggression at the same time as building your muscle tone. You try.'

We stand there, flexing our biceps.

'You can even do it like this.' She drops her arms to her sides and starts clenching and unclenching her fists, like she's picking up invisible suitcases. 'When you're walking along, or sitting on the bus. You can even do it in class. I find it terrific. You try.'

We pick up and drop our imaginary suitcases. It's weird, but it is sort of relaxing.

Ms Pewty smiles. 'There you are. So. Next time you feel angry or anxious about Mr Berkhoff—just flex. I find it also helps to think of something nice. And, Ian, before you go, I have to say this. The things you do to Mr Berkhoff all show amazing sporting skills. I know you think they're flukes, but it can't do any harm to see whether you do have hidden sporting talents. So. How about you come and do some training with the football team some time?'

I nod in agreement so I can get away. The only members of the football team that I know are all psychopaths.

'Now off you go.'

I put my bag on my back and head off. There might be something to this flexing business, so I keep picking up and dropping my imaginary suitcases as I go. It's a bit hard to flex as you're walking because your arms have to stay stiff. In fact, catching sight of my reflection in the science block doors I look a bit like an ape man. But if it will break the jinx I'll do it. Although, according to Ms Pewty, it's not a jinx. It's just that I hate Berkhoff. Which is absolutely true. I remember I have to think of something nice.

I think of mud cake. Then I notice Ms Pewty coming out of one of the science block doors. She's talking earnestly to someone. I can't see who.

Oh God, it's Berkhoff.

I freeze, then frantically start flexing my hanging arms. He's chatting to Ms Pewty. He's even smiling—which, with his black eye, is pretty horrible to look at. I notice he's got a huge bandaid on his hand.

I walk off very slowly, still flexing, thinking of mud cake. I can feel the cleaners looking at me, but I keep going. As I get to the school gates, I take one last look at Berkhoff. He's still okay.

I run like crazy. I have to put as much distance between myself and Berkhoff as possible. Along the esplanade, past the shopping mall. I keep running all the way home, then stop in surprise.

The footpath outside our shop is completely packed with motorbikes and old men in black leather biker suits, all shouting.

Right in the middle, shouting louder than anyone, still in his blue singlet and shorts, is Syd. He's up a stepladder organising the others to hang a string of yellow and black flags all around our shop. Of course. Tomorrow we're opening. How could I forget?

But where are Mum and Dad in all this? The crowd parts and I see Dad encircled by gigantic bikers. He's chatting and laughing, holding a big bunch of yellow balloons.

'Hey, Ian! The best bit of luck. Turns out the colours we chose for the shop are the same colours as the Yarradindi

Cannibals. They're lending us their decorations.'

And as I look, I see that on one side all of the balloons have got YARRADINDI CANNIBALS printed on them. They also have a black skull.

A skull? To advertise a health food shop? What planet does Dad live on? How has Mum allowed this to happen?

At that moment there's a crash of china. It's followed by a high-pitched scream, and Ripper comes shooting out of the shop at two hundred k's an hour. We freeze in amazement.

Dad gasps, 'Oh my God, the muffins!'

Chapter 9

We run through the shop into the kitchen.
The place is full of black smoke. Dad got
so involved with the Cannibals that he
forgot he was supposed to be watching
two dozen muffins in the oven while Mum
wrote the menu cards in the living room.
This is half of the shop's supply for tomorrow. The other half, which were cooling
on the table, have been knocked to the
floor and eaten by Ripper.

Granny Pocky runs in, saying she
heard the scream. She's furious with Syd
for distracting Dad, and goes into a
general rave about the incompetence of
men generally. Every time she moves her
arms about, the crocodile down her cleavage changes position. She says she and Syd
will stay all night to help Dad fix up the

shop while Mum and me make more muffins.

Syd offers to shoot Ripper. Mum says that's not necessary. Dad keeps apologising. Mum refuses to talk to him.

Mum and I clear up the floor and start cooking. I measure out all the flour and stuff, and wash up the utensils as she finishes with them. Dad comes in to apologise again and he and Mum have a huge row. It turns out that as well as forgetting the muffins, Dad misread Mum's handwriting and accidentally ordered seven cartons of extremely hot Japanese wasabi horseradish instead of one little box. The distributors won't take it back, so now we have enough wasabi to last Yarradindi for decades. Also, Terry Pocky has still not turned up to install the shelves.

Dad turns the argument back on Mum. He says that at least the wasabi is not perishable, unlike the stacks of speckled, cruddy-looking organically grown fruit and vegetables that Mum bought from some old hippy.

This fight carries on all evening. I watch as I load up the aromatherapy display. The fight stops when Syd or Granny Pocky enters the room and flares up as soon as they leave. It stops completely when Terry Pocky arrives with Troy to fix up the shelves. Except that Terry happens to mention that he saw the old hippy coming into the shop, and asks if we knew the guy has memory blackouts and fleas. And they're off again.

Terry's T-shirt reads: DON'T BE A NUTTER, LET POCKY FIX YOUR GUTTER.

I have to look after Troy for Terry. Troy is incredibly violent and his nose runs. He's got this little plastic toy chainsaw that makes a whirring noise when you pull a string. At one point he gets his head stuck between the banisters on our stairs. I'm tempted to leave him there.

At one o'clock in the morning the shelves are finished and we start loading them. Mum remembers that she has six hanging baskets of ferns on chains to attach to the ceiling in the little café section of the shop. She and Terry have a huge battle about how low to hang them. Terry reckons if they're hung as low as Mum wants, people will be hitting their heads on them and using them to stub out their cigarettes. Mum says low baskets create a relaxing, rainforest atmosphere and, in any case, the café is no smoking.

Dad is in the middle of it all, trying to make peace. Every time Mum goes out, Terry lifts the baskets higher up the chains. Every time Mum comes in, she lowers them.

I go to bed and leave them all to it. Moving here has been a totally bad idea. I drift into terrible nightmares about Berkhoff coming to get me and the Ratbag Criminal Element coming to get me and Ms Pewty preventing me from getting away by making me flex all around the oval. The oval turns into our shop and the Ratbag Criminal Element is coming to drag me outside. Just as they're about to jump me, the clock radio goes off.

It's a great relief. But the dream has set me thinking. What happens if the Ratbag Criminal Element does come to the shop? I refuse to think about it. I do a few flexes. I take my morning vitamins.

When I get downstairs my parents are already up and putting the finishing touches to the shop. It's amazing. You'd never know the place looked like a rubbish heap about six hours ago. The baskets are hung low on their chains. Mum and Dad are all happy again, chatting cheerfully. They're both wearing black aprons. Dad's rearranging the vitamin pill containers on Terry's shelves. Terry's actually put them up a bit high for us, since we're all so little, but Dad says it's a good use of space.

Mum's bustling about in the café section. On the counter there's a sign saying SPECIAL: TWO FOR THE PRICE OF ONE attached to a box of stuff in tubes. It's the hot Japanese wasabi Dad over-ordered.

All is going well. Dad strikes up 'All You Need is Soy'. This is the Beatles' song 'All You Need is Love' with the word 'soy' substituted for 'love'. Mum and I join in. It's fun. There's nearly a total disaster when the top of the food blender flies off while Mum is making carrot juice. Luckily Dad's close to the switch and flicks it off immediately.

Meanwhile, despite myself, I keep thinking of what I'll do if the Ratbag Criminal Element turns up. I work out that if I stand behind the aromatherapy display, I can get a good view of the street in both directions without being seen. This means that if I see them coming I can either duck in the storeroom or, in a desperate situation, hide below the counter near the cash register.

Countdown to eight-thirty: opening time.

Mum suddenly notices I'm wearing my old T-shirt and sends me up to get changed. As soon as I come down, she notices my nails and sends me up to scrub my hands. When I reappear there's still a tiny bit of dirt in my left thumbnail and she goes utterly ballistic and sends me off for the third time.

Finally I'm clean enough for her and she gives me this black apron to wear. It reaches my ankles. I say I'm not going to wear it. She says she's not going to give me any pocket money unless I do. She puts it over my head, folds it over a few times at the waist and ties me in from behind. This way, while I do look as if I have an incredibly fat stomach, I can at least walk. Unfortunately, I can't bend over at all.

Luckily, Dad comes in from the back of the shop and says, 'For God's sake, Jan, take it off him. He looks like something out of Snow White and the Seven Dwarfs.'

Mum holds out for a while but finally gives in and takes it off me. We all have a final practice with the cash register. By this time, it's eight-fifteen and an elderly couple are standing outside peering in.

We're inside peering out. Mum and Dad discuss whether we should open early. Mum wants to. Dad says it would look unprofessional. The suspense is terrible. Finally, at eight twenty-five, Mum gives this strangled roaring noise, dashes to the door and unlocks it.

It turns out that the old people are selling raffle tickets. Dad beckons me over, leans down and whispers, 'Don't tell Mum, but . . .' He checks she's not listening. 'There's a rat in the storeroom.'

Chapter 10

While Mum buys five tickets to win a complete lady's or gentleman's lawn bowling outfit, Dad whispers an explanation. The rat turned up two days ago and is refusing to eat the bait Dad put down for it. Rather than give Mum something else to worry about, Dad has told her the rat is dead. He's worked out a solution with Syd and Terry. At some stage today Syd and Terry will secretly set up special traps. These consist of rat-bait pellets mashed together with beer and cornflakes and placed inside big empty cocoa tins. They are an ancient Pocky remedy guaranteed to work. The cocoa tin, as Dad points out, provides a ready-made coffin.

We're interrupted by Mum coming over to the cash register. She's beaming from her first sale, which is two bars of herbal soap (actually, they sell for less than the cost of the raffle tickets, but who's counting). As the old people leave, Dad gives me a high five and kisses Mum on the cheek. Mid-kiss, his eyes flick anxiously to the storeroom.

I suddenly remember the Ratbags. I have to take precautions. So, while Mum and Dad are chatting, I stroll over to the aromatherapy display, then quickly duck down. This is excellent. I can see the street through the display. I can even move up and down, as long as I keep myself bent over. A few people come in and look at me a bit oddly, but I pretend not to notice. An old man with shorts up to his chest just stands there and stares. I'm practising walking doubled over when I hear Mum whispering, 'Ian, are you all right?'

She's come up right next to me so the old man won't hear.

'What? I'm fine.'

'Why are you bent over like that?'

'I'm not.'

I straighten my back but keep my legs bent. This makes my bum stick out at the back like a gorilla, but it means I can't be seen from the street. I fold my arms and try to look casual.

She stares at me in a puzzled way then moves off. I immediately crouch down again. I peer through the display. All clear. Then my stomach does a backflip. The Ratbag Criminal Element are across the road. They're looking in the window of the electrical shop.

Go into the electrical shop!

They don't. They slouch on to the music shop next door and start looking through a display of CDs.

Go into the music shop!

At that moment, Dad comes in from the back of the shop. He's carrying a box full of groceries and a cardboard sign advertising soy milk.

'Here Ian. Stick this sign in the window.'

I look desperately across the road. The Ratbags are still looking at the CDs.

I pretend to be busy with the aroma-therapy stuff.

I say calmly, 'Can Mum do it?'

Mum's buttering muffins. She smiles tightly at the old man and says (sweetly, but like she could murder me), 'No I can't. You do it, Ian.'

There's nothing else for it. I bend my knees and keep my back straight. Like an ape man, I scuttle across to Dad, grab the sign, stick it in the window and go scuttling back.

'Oh, and do this one as well, will you.'

The Ratbag Criminal Element is crossing the road. I'm going to die. I go scuttling back and snatch the sign.

Mum says, 'Why are you walking like that? Oh wait a minute, here's another one . . .'

No! No . . .!

The Ratbag Criminal Element enters the shop. I freeze.

The old man says, 'That boy's constipated.'

I suddenly realise I am still squatting like a gorilla. I stand up. At the same time the old man leaves, Mum walks off into the storeroom, and Dad hisses, 'Oh no, the rat!' and dashes off to distract her.

I'm on my own. The chief smiles, strolls over and leans down until his pimply face is close to my own. He glances over his shoulder to check he's not being seen.

He whispers, 'How much for the pills?'

Chapter 11

I blink.

He glances round again. 'Come on, man. You're popping them all day.'

I can feel my eyebrows shoot up. 'You mean ... my vitamins?'

'Vitamins! Oh yeah, sure, "vitamins!" '

They all start going 'Vitamins' and chuckling knowingly.

'No, they are! They're Teenage Energy Pills. With odourless garlic.'

The chief bursts out laughing. 'Sure, garlic's what made you take out Cobbett and Berkhoff. It was garlic that made you kick a ball halfway to Melbourne. Fine, man, give me ten bucks' worth of ...' he smirks, 'Teenage Energy Pills!'

I stand there, trying to take in the fact that they think my vitamins are giving me some kind of superhuman strength. It's ridiculous. But it's also terrifying because as soon as they work out the truth they'll be back to get me. Mum appears. She smiles professionally, puts a bottle of Teenage Energy Pills in the chief's hand and says, 'That's nine dollars ninety-five. Take a maximum of five a day, and drink at least nine glasses of water to protect your kidneys.'

The chief accepts his change, smiles conspiratorially at me, says, 'You're all right, man,' and slouches out, leading the others.

Now, common sense tells me I should find a hiding place, preferably on another continent. But I'm frozen to the spot. Being picked on by Clint and Cunningham was bad enough. Now I'm in league with the Year 12 Mafia. In fact, as the Ratbags will see it, I'm ripping off the Year 12 Mafia. And I've seen enough gangster movies to know what happens to people who rip off the Mob.

With sinking heart, I watch the three Ratbags cross the road and slip down an alleyway. The chief opens the bottle and solemnly offers it round. Each takes a pill and swallows. Of course, nothing happens. Nothing will happen. Nothing will happen for three hours, at which time they will come back and beat me to a pulp. At that moment, just as I'm wearily visualising myself getting hammered into the dried fruit counter, something weird happens.

Playfully, the chief gives one of the others a shove. It's only a little shove, but the guy stumbles backwards, trips and falls over. When he gets up he's holding his wrist and crying.

You'd expect the other two to be concerned about their friend, but they're not. They laugh in surprise and look triumphantly at the pill bottle. The chief sees me standing in our doorway. He grins, punches the air and yells, 'Those vitamins, man. They're dynamite! I wrecked his wrist!'

At that moment, another group of tough-looking Year 12s comes up to see what's wrong. I watch the chief explaining and pointing to the bottle. They all reach to take one, but he snatches the bottle away and points towards our shop.

In less time than it takes me to whiz back behind the aromatherapy display, the four tough-looking Year 12 boys hurry excitedly into the shop, wink and smirk at me, and buy a bottle of Teenage Energy Pills. On their way out, they bump into a group of extremely tough-looking girls, who do the same thing. Soon there's a steady stream of frighteningly aggro-looking kids all buying pills and greeting me like I'm one of their own.

Terrific. Now they'll all want to beat me up.

But Mum and Dad are thrilled. Dad cracks jokes with all the kids as he puts their pills into bags. Mum gets all chatty. She advises them to supplement the pills with a lot of water, fresh fruit and vege-tables. She explains how I take the pills and it's the secret of my good health. At this, the kids all smile knowingly at me.

Mum comments to Dad on how polite the local kids are. She doesn't realise they think she's some kind of female drug lord.

In between we get a few other custom-ers. A cranky old vicar comes in to get some cream for his athlete's foot. One old lady is in for ages talking about having her gallstones out. Dad's pretending he's really interested until she tells him she's kept her gallstones in a bottle under the sink and offers to bring them in.

A dentist called Vicki fronts up. She wants to check whether we sell fluoride-free toothpaste. She suggests we refuse to sell people normal toothpaste. She reckons the best thing is for everyone to clean their teeth with freshly-cut eucalyptus twigs and salt, provided free by us as a community service. Mum smiles and says she'll think about it. Dad reckons Vicki must be the busiest dentist in town, since all her patients would have terrible teeth.

But mostly the older locals just stand outside gawking, then walk on. That's not counting the Pockys. About twenty Pockys of all ages come in at various times to wish us good luck, praise Terry's shelves and make jokes about the vegeburger. None of them buys anything. Then Terry himself comes in to wish us good luck, admire his shelves and make jokes about the vege-burger. His T-shirt reads: DON'T START TO WHINGE, LET POCKY FIX THAT HINGE. He's got Troy with him. Mum makes me offer Troy a spotty, organically grown pear.

Troy says, 'Nick off'.

Meanwhile, the street outside is filling up with kids whooping and belting each other and doing suicidal things on skate-boards under the imaginary influence of

Teenage Energy Pills. Mum smiles approvingly. She says that's what's so nice about the country. The kids know how to entertain themselves.

Clint and Cunningham go past, leaping in the air like madmen and popping three of our balloons. It's hard to tell whether they're behaving normally or whether they think Teenage Energy Pills are giving them superhuman powers.

By ten o'clock we've sold forty bottles of Teenage Energy Pills. By eleven o'clock it's fifty, and by eleven-thirty we've sold out.

Mum and Dad are pleased. They like the fact that the local kids are so into good health.

Mum turns to me. 'See, Ian! You thought everyone at school would laugh at Teenage Energy Pills, didn't you! Life's full of surprises!'

She doesn't know how right she is.

I bury myself in the washing-up to mull over the day's events. I can't believe the kids in this place. How could they even begin to think that vitamin pills could be drugs? I suppose a health food shop seems so weird to these people that they don't know what to expect. I sigh. I check my watch. How much longer can it be before the Mob comes back to get me? I wish I was back in Sydney. I pass the time by remembering good stuff I did with my friends. Finn and me going skateboarding ... The time Sam bet me I wouldn't jump off the ten metre board ...

Syd provides a bit of a distraction by turning up with his biker friend, Skull. Skull parks his three-wheeled Harley Davidson on the footpath outside. He's got a big grey moustache and a huge belly hanging over the belt of his leather trousers. He's wearing a black leather jacket with a lot of studs on it. He's bald on top, but the long grey hair around his ears is tied back in a ponytail. He's on a low-cholesterol diet, so he's really interested in health foods. He tells me that his doctor said every time he eats egg and chips his heart is begging him for mercy.

Mum recommends freshly squeezed orange juice and an oat bran muffin, plus some pills for his digestion made out of a herb called cat's claw. I prepare the food. Skull gulps down the herbal pills and wolfs his food. He announces he can feel it doing him good. Particularly the dead cat. Syd bellows out an order for one of Mum's soy milk banana smoothies. I make it in the blender for him. He tastes it and nearly gags. But he says it's top tucker, and tells Dad he's a lucky beggar to have Mum cooking for him. He eats a couple of Skull's cat's claw pills. He whispers to Dad that the rat traps are ready to go in as soon as Terry finds two more cocoa tins.

Terry turns up ten minutes later carrying a bulging sportsbag. Dad tells me to distract Mum while he, Terry and Syd slip into the storeroom and set the traps. I get Mum going on to Skull about the benefits of oat bran. I'm so involved with this that I don't notice Andy Bogle leaning against the deep freeze, rolling his lips. He says, 'They'll kill you when they find out those pills are only vitamins.'

I make a real effort to look calm. I need to sound incredibly scathing. I do my best impersonation of Caroline Dillinger and sneer, 'Who says they're not?'

'Your mum.'

Go for cool. I half-close my eyes like the Ratbags. I drawl, 'You seem to know a lot about it.'

'I do. It's called the placebo effect, that's *pla-see-bo*. It's well known to medical researchers. It's when you give someone a pill that they think is a drug and they react as if it is. So, for example, you can tell sick people you're giving them a new, powerful drug and they'll get better—even if the pills you give them are only aspirin. It's the power of the mind.'

He's too clever by half.

I go, 'What's it to you?'

He stares at me, rotates his lips and says, 'Well, for the purposes of an experiment, I was thinking of telling them.'

Chapter 12

I can't stop myself. Before I know it, I've muttered an excuse, dashed out of the shop and set off in a panic down the street. I'm trying desperately to be like Dad and look on the bright side. The bright side is that I am no longer getting wedgies at school and Cobbett doesn't seem to be suing us. The other side is that the Year 12 Mafia think I'm a drug dealer and Andy Bogle is threatening to dob me in.

How did I get into all this? As for Bogle ...! I should have thumped him. I get furious. I go across the park punching the air and imagining it's his head. Then I pick up a stone and throw it. It makes me feel better. Bloody Andy Bogle. I pick up another one and chuck it hard at a park bench.

I pick up a huge rock and hurl it with all my might into some trees.

There's a yell. A man on a bike comes careering out through the trees and crashes into a camellia bush.

It's Berkhoff.

I can feel my mouth hanging open. How can Berkhoff have been there? There was nobody there two seconds before! This is spooky. It's more than spooky, it's terrifying.

I run like mad across the park, ducking behind the trees so Berkhoff won't see me. When I'm far enough away, I look out from behind a tree trunk. Berkhoff's rubbing his shoulder and pulling this agonised face and swearing. He's been joined by Ms Pewty, dressed in a gleaming lycra bike outfit with a really short top. She's putting her bike on the ground. Now she's checking his shoulder. I don't think they've seen me, but Berkhoff keeps looking round in a furious way between swearwords. When he bends over to check out his damaged bike, I slip off across the park and into the streets beyond.

This is a nightmare! What's happening to me? I didn't even see Berkhoff, so there's no way I could have accidentally willed it to happen.

Then a thought occurs to me. I'm cursed.

I stop in my tracks. That's it. Some ... *thing* has put a curse on me. Some Force resents me for coming to Yarradindi to set up a health food shop. I mean, really, the people the Force should be getting are my mum and dad, not me. They're the ones setting up the shop. Still, who said forces of evil had to be logical?

I dismiss the idea. It's stupid. I start walking again, then stop, because the idea won't go away. Maybe it's not so stupid. Maybe I've found the cause of all my problems. My mind is racing. I try to remember a book I read about some little kid being taken over by Forces of Evil. Are there any resemblances? As far as I can recall, being taken over by forces of evil seemed to involve a lot of talking in weird voices and frothing at the mouth. I'm certainly not frothing at the mouth (not that I'm aware of, anyway), but has my voice changed?

I say 'Ian Rude' a few times, with different expressions. An old lady gives me a weird look so I pretend to be coughing until she's gone. Then I try again. My voice doesn't seem to have changed, but then, would I know?

The little kid didn't know. You'd think he'd have twigged that something odd was going on when he woke up to find people wearing wreaths of garlic and holding giant crucifixes peeking out from behind his bedroom curtains, but apparently not.

A tough-looking kid flies past me on a skateboard. It reminds me of the Ratbag Criminal Element and the fact that any minute I'll probably be jumped. I walk on. This curse thing is just not fair. If I have to injure people, why can't I choose who gets it? Why can't I make rocks fall on people like the Ratbags—or Clint and Cunningham? That would be good. I could give them wedgies by telepathy.

Perhaps I can.

The point is, if I have developed some strange power—and I'm pretty sure I haven't, but let's just say for the moment I have—why fight it?

Why not give myself over to the Power . . .?

After all, who knows what I could do if I concentrate on using my powers! Instead of being frightened of the Ratbag

Criminal Element, I could annihilate them. Or—and this is even crazier—I could become their leader! I gasp. I could probably kill people if I put my mind to it! I could murder Berkhoff!

'Ian?'

I jump with surprise. It's Ms Pewty, wheeling her bike.

'Are you all right?'

I stammer, 'Yes, Ms Pewty.'

I stare at her. Her eyes look all weak and odd because she's not wearing her glasses. But what's really noticeable is the short, clinging top she's wearing. It's made of the most incredibly gleaming, silvery lycra stuff. It makes her boobs look spectacular. They look like they're made out of chrome.

I try not to look, which is really hard since my eyes are on an exact level with them.

'Are you sure? Why are your eyes so large and glassy?'

I can't really say I'm caught between considering a career as a homicidal maniac and perving her gleaming boobs.

'Look Ian, I wonder if I could have a word. It *was* you who threw a rock at Mr Berkhoff just now, wasn't it?'

This is so unfair! I plead, 'It was an accident!'

'Ian, have you been flexing?'

'No, Ms Pewty.'

She stares at me anxiously and sighs. Those boobs are amazing. You can see your reflection in them.

'Ian, flexing will help you get rid of your anger. And so will exercise. Football, for example, as I've already said. You must join the team, Ian. With the throwing and kicking skills you've been showing you're probably a natural.'

I struggle to concentrate. Ms Pewty's frowning anxiously as she fastens her crash helmet.

'Anyway, think about it. Now, are you sure you're okay?'

'Yes, Ms Pewty.'

She really is kind. I remember what she said about my subconscious mind causing the problems with Berkhoff. That's much more likely than being cursed or filled with fiendish powers. In fact, the more I think about that, the dumber it seems. I cheer up.

She smiles briefly, then frowns. 'I'd better go. I've got guests for dinner. Remember, at the first sign of stress, breathe deeply and flex.'

I smile gratefully. 'Yes, Ms Pewty.'

I look her firmly in the eye to avoid the boobs. She swings herself onto the saddle. The boobs bounce, shining, into position. She frowns anxiously at me again.

'Are you quite sure you don't want me to phone your parents to pick you up?'

'I'm fine.'

'Positive?'

What a nice person. I smile and nod my head.

I say, 'Go home to your breasts.'

Chapter 13

'Guests! Guests!'

I'm dying! She tosses a puzzled glance at me like she's not sure what I said, and puts her foot on the pedal.

'Bye, Ian. See you at school.'

That's it, I'm cursed. The Thing is doing this to me. But what *is* It? Is It someone who used to live in our house? Someone who was murdered there? I hope nobody was murdered in my room.

That really gives me the creeps. Supposing some ghost is after me! How do you get rid of a ghost?

And then I see it. Like a message from On High—a church. And outside, bending over picking up ice-cream wrappers and junk chucked over the fence, is a vicar. But it's not any old vicar. It's the vicar who was in our shop getting stuff for his athlete's foot. Relief washes over me. I can ask him to exorcise the ghost.

I give a little sob and hurry up to him, calling, 'Excuse me!'

He looks up, squinting. I grin and open my mouth to explain. But words fail me. What do I say? It's a bit hard to introduce exorcism into the conversation. Especially to a man wearing flower-patterned gardening gloves and holding a bundle of old chip wrappers.

He looks at me. I look at him. My mouth is opening and closing. How can I introduce the subject? I think of Dad and go for jovial casualness. I beam, fold my arms and say, 'So then! How's the athlete's foot?'

Oh no, I've done it again!

'What did you say?'

I stammer, 'No! Please! I think I'm cursed.'

He's furious. 'You're the boy from the health food shop.'

'I need an exorcism . . .'

'You assaulted the Principal and Mr Berkhoff.'

'That's the problem. I have unbelievable strength!'

'I'll give you unbelievable strength!' He raises his broom in the air. 'You were one of the hooligans who stuck chewing gum in the water fountain by the church hall, weren't you? Yes, I recognise you!'

And then, like a complete psycho, he shakes his broom and comes chasing after me with it. Every time I shout out that I didn't stick chewing gum anywhere but I do need an exorcism, he yells, calls me a vandal and tries to whack me. He chases me all around the churchyard and up to the church hall before I manage to duck off down an alleyway next to the sign saying COMFORT YE MY PEOPLE. I run like crazy then double back through the shopping mall.

Lost him.

I sink miserably down onto a seat next to the new Federation-style bandstand. The people in this town are all insane. Still, how can I have said that stuff about his athlete's foot? How can I have ruined my one chance of salvation? I glance at my watch. It's now three hours since the last bottle of Teenage Energy Pills was sold, so probably only minutes from my destruction.

I sigh. I consider my options. I could

103

tell Mum and Dad. I could run away. I could go to Finn's place in Sydney and we could go to the police together. But what do you say? That you think you're in the grip of supernatural powers? I'd end up in the loony bin—which has the advantage of putting me out of reach of the Ratbags, I suppose. But not much else.

No, I have to deal with this. I have to find out what it is that's influencing me so I can give the police some proof. Who would know about local ghosts? In particular, who would know about ghosts in our house? Syd and Granny would. Now there's an idea. I'll go there straight away. I'll pretend I've got a school assignment on ghosts and supernatural occurrences in the neighbourhood and pump them for everything they know.

I glance around to check for lurking Ratbags. All clear. I set off for Syd's the back way.

Syd's not in, but Granny Pocky throws up her arms to greet me. The crocodile down her cleavage bulges one eye and rolls in leathery wrinkles. The wild pig now has an umbrella hanging from one tusk. I start asking questions straight away, but Granny shuts me up and leads me into the living room. The wrestling's on TV. It's a bout between some huge guy in a balaclava helmet called the Masked Invader and an equally huge guy covered in tattoos called Mauler McGee. Granny explains that she's got a bet on Mauler to lose. She's using a little bottle of our aromatherapy stuff to calm her nerves.

As she sits down, I ask whether anyone was murdered in our place and Granny gives an agonised shout. For a second I think it's because I've hit on some horrible truth, but in fact it's because Mauler has just thrown the Masked Invader to the canvas and jumped on his chest. She takes a good long sniff of the aromatherapy bottle and asks me to repeat the question.

It's hopeless. Every time I try to ask a question, Mauler does something terrible to the Masked Invader and Granny Pocky starts yelling, 'Get him, you fat wuss!' between calming sniffs. After about ten minutes I get out of her that our place was only built thirty years ago, nobody's been murdered or even died in it, and the couple who built it are now happily retired on the Gold Coast.

When I ask if there's any reason at all why a local ghost might be upset because our place is a health food shop, I have to wait for ages while Mauler and the Masked Invader chase each other round the ring, bouncing wildly off the ropes. But once that's over and the Invader has thrown Mauler out into the spectators, Granny Pocky takes a sniff and remembers that the father of the old lady who used to live in our place did actually hate green vegetables. But, she adds, she doesn't think he'd return from the dead about it.

I give up. I watch the Masked Invader being declared the winner then trudge off down the back lane to our place to meet my doom. I miss Sydney. I miss Finn. I miss school being normal. Most of all I miss being normal myself. I sigh heavily, glance over our fence—and see Dad sitting astride Skull's Harley and chatting to a group of Cannibals sprawled about on the grass.

I'm too weary even to say hello. Mum's clearing up the shop. Our takings are about a hundred and fifty dollars, which is not good. But then it's only our first day. I help. At first, I keep glancing out the window expecting the Ratbags. But they don't come, so I give up. I'm too tired to care.

As I go into the storeroom I notice a faint smell of beer and see the glint of a cocoa tin high on a shelf. Poor rat. I know what it's like to be hunted.

We have dinner, cooked by Dad. It features dollops of the Japanese wasabi he overordered, which turns out to be so hot it feels like it's sending the entire contents of your skull into meltdown. By eight o'clock I'm in my room, getting ready for bed.

I look round my room, wondering whether there is actually some Being here who's making my life so miserable. If there is, I'm strangely unscared of It. Maybe that means It's already got me in its grasp.

I go (all tough), 'All right. If you're in here, give me a sign!'

Nothing happens.

I say, 'Well rack off, then.'

Nothing happens.

I say, 'Dork.'

I feel a bit better.

Chapter 14

The next morning I wake up late and immediately start to imagine the Thing is under my bed. I steel myself and sneak a look. Nothing. That means the only thing I have to worry about is the army of kids who want to beat me up. Great. I decide the best way to avoid them is to stay in my bedroom all day. For that I'll need food.

I enter the kitchen to find there's been a snowstorm inside and Troy is marooned in the middle of a dirty snowdrift. It's not really a snowdrift. It's actually three giant plastic sacks of popcorn that Mum was planning to use as biodegradable padding around the bottles of Teenage Energy Pills that we're hoping to sell through mail order. Troy's slumped in the middle of it, looking as if he's about to be sick. He's got bits of popcorn stuck all round his mouth. He looks at me, goes 'Ni . . .' But he just can't get the words out.

As I'm staring at him, a tall skinny man with long hair and a beard stumbles backwards through the door. He's carrying a big cardboard box of speckled, midget oranges. He's wearing a strange baggy suit with trousers that end halfway up his hairy calves. It looks like it's made of tea towels. He cracks his head on a hanging basket, swears feebly, looks down at the box and murmurs, 'Was that three boxes . . . or four?'

He notices Troy and the popcorn. He frowns and blinks, then says thoughtfully, 'Whoa! A kid in an ocean of popcorn . . .'

I can hear Mum and Dad quarrelling before the door even opens. Mum bursts in shouting, 'A shelf should not fall down the day after it's installed! A shelf is *designed* to have things placed on top of it . . .' But, seeing the popcorn, she stops dead.

Dad's shouting, 'Look, Terry's going to fix it, he . . .' But, seeing the popcorn, *he* stops dead.

Terry Pocky comes in behind them. He's saying, 'Well, a course, if you're going to put stuff on *top* of them . . .'

He sees Troy and the popcorn. He gives a shout of laughter. 'Struth mate! You won't need anything else to eat today! Don't worry, Jan, we'll clear it up.'

Mum draws her breath in sharply, turns on her heel and storms out.

Dad, Terry and I exchange looks. Tea Towel man nods his head wisely. 'That's good. She's giving vent.'

Dad rubs his hands together, grins round at us all and says, typically, 'This won't take us a minute.'

Of course, it actually takes hours. Only Dad and I are doing it. Terry goes off to fix the shelves that have fallen down. Every time he comes through the kitchen, he gives a big tut, says 'Women!' in an exasperated way, and asks what you expect shelves to do if you put stuff on top of them. Troy is strapped into the cafe's highchair, where he gets greener and greener. After half an hour he goes to sleep with his mouth open. After an hour he stirs in his sleep, gives an enormous burp, sighs, and starts to snore.

At first I'm totally on edge worrying about when the Ratbags are going to appear. Then I give up worrying. To be more precise, I accept my fate. Whenever it will occur. Tea Towel man turns out to be Mick, the hippy, who supplies us with organically grown fruit. He starts out helping to pack the popcorn back into some sacks, but he's incredibly slow and keeps trying to turn the conversation to Emotions. He also keeps cracking his head on the hanging baskets.

Finally, Dad sends him off to check he's given us the right number of boxes. This is good, because he's stuck there counting, forgetting what he's counted and starting again, which keeps him away from us.

Dad and I work together. He explains that Mum's a bit tense because she's found out that the whole town now believes our shop and cafe is a bikie meeting place. This wouldn't be a problem except that while the Yarradindi Cannibals think of themselves as a fun-loving, community-minded social group, the locals think of them as a pack of homicidal maniacs. For example, Syd had told Dad this really nice story about how, every Christmas, the Cannibals go to Yarradindi Retirement Village and provide the residents with free motorbike rides up and down the freeway.

Syd had said it always warms his heart to hear their happy shouts and yells as he hits 120 k's.

The story Mum and Dad have now heard from a lady who lives there is that every Christmas the Cannibals descend on the village, refuse to take no for an answer and drag off old people, screaming. Dad says that Mum's also upset because Syd didn't tell her that Skull's got a metal plate in the back of his head and gets road rage at the full moon.

As Dad points out, that is, after all, pretty personal stuff.

By the time we're finished it's late afternoon. Dad makes a pot of tea for everyone and gets me to take a cup to Mum as a peace offering. She takes it, but tuts angrily, and says, 'Your father ...!'

I go back to the kitchen. I sit down to have my tea with Dad, Terry and Mick. Syd and Skull join us. I look round at them all. Dad and Skull are listening to Terry, who's doing tae kwon do whoops and waving his arms to illustrate his last tournament. Syd's roaring approval of Terry. Mick is staring at Terry and nodding his head wisely. Why aren't any of them sensible?

Mick leans over me, smiling. He says, 'You see? What Terry does is *connect*.'

As I'm looking at him, a speck of something springs out of his beard, lands on the table, bounces high in the air and lands on the floor.

The day ends without any kids arriving to get me. Oh well. They'll come soon enough. Dinner features more Japanese wasabi. I go to bed, congratulating myself on my state of grim acceptance. I wish the ghost goodnight. Nothing happens. Maybe It's planning to get me in my sleep. So be it.

I've lost the power to worry.

Chapter 15

Unfortunately, the power to worry reappears in full force the next morning when I set out for school and realise a mob of the toughest Year 7s is marching behind me like a guard of honour. It's unnerving. I pretend not to notice. All the way there I see older kids whispering and pointing.

As I come in the school gates my path is blocked by Clint and Cunningham. Cunningham looks round excitedly and wheezes, 'You gotta come with us.'

This is it. My heart is pounding. We head off towards the sports field. They're taking me a long way from the school buildings so they can beat me to a pulp at their leisure.

But then I notice that we're heading for the smoking tree. I don't know whether to be relieved or even more worried. The smoking tree is where all the Year 12 smokers hang out, while a pack of slaves like Clint and Cunningham keep watch for teachers. The smell of smoke is really strong and there are cigarette butts to a depth of about ten centimetres all around the roots. You wonder whether the tree itself is actually addicted. It probably gives off carbon monoxide instead of oxygen. It probably spends all weekend shaking its leaves and gasping for a cigarette.

As we approach, I notice the Ratbags lounging against the tree, smoking and looking serious. I prepare myself for the worst. The chief raises his pimply face. I gulp. He smiles. What? He's smiling instead of ordering my execution? What's going on here?

He points to himself and the other Ratbags and murmurs, 'Darren, Derrin and Kurt.'

He looks furtively over his shoulder. 'I can move as many pills as you can get me.'

I stare at him. I feel like I'm in an episode of some crime show. Is everyone in this town completely mad?

Darren, the chief, explains that the demand for Teenage Energy Pills is now so enormous that he and the other Ratbags are already selling individual pills to high-paying customers. Apparently, sales skyrocketed after Dylan Pocky took three pills and broke the Yarradindi record for holding your breath while sticking your head in a rock pool.

He wants me to hijack the next shipment of pills when they're delivered to the shop. That way, the Ratbag Criminal Element and I have complete control over the market. I smile weakly and say, 'Look, I have to tell you. They're only vitamin pills.'

He stares back at me, smiles, and says, 'That's just the way we want it.' He holds out his hand for me to shake. 'Good to have you in town.'

I shake it, but tell him it would be really difficult for me to pinch an entire consignment of Teenage Energy Pills without anyone noticing. He turns to Derrin and Kurt. They step aside to discuss it. They come back after a few moments to tell me that I'm not to worry about hijacking the Teenage Energy Pills for now. My job is to tell them when the pills arrive.

At that moment a whistle blows from

the other side of the field and someone shouts 'Ian!' Oh God, it's Ms Pewty! But at least it provides a distraction. Darren, Derrin and Kurt hastily stub out their cigarettes. I stuff my bottle of Teenage Energy Pills into Darren's hand and hurry off towards the school buildings trying to work out my options.

The only ray of hope here is that Bogle clearly hasn't told anyone the truth. But how long can the placebo effect work? People start calling out to me to buy Teenage Energy Pills. I ignore them and dash into the library building. I dump down my bag and slump miserably against the wall next to the entrance, which is two swing doors with porthole windows.

As I glance at them, Andy Bogle's demented face looms up on the other side of a porthole. He grins and presses his face against the glass so his nose and lips balloon out all fleshy and disgusting. He is so irritating. If he comes in here I'll thump him. Then I remember he knows about the vitamins. I'll have to be nice to him. I take a look at him. I cannot be nice to him.

I grab my bag and stride off out of the building.

'Ian!'

The nerd's following me! I ignore him. He keeps following me across the quad.

He says, 'I think you're giving off a force field and Berkhoff's allergic to it. The deal is, you help me with my science competition project and I don't tell about the pills. But if you won't . . .'

He mimes a throat being slit, grins, and walks off, bumping into a Year 11 boy who sidles up to me. The Year 11 gulps and whispers, 'You got anything to make hair grow in your armpits?'

At that moment, Berkhoff drives his red Barina round the corner, catches sight of me and whacks straight into the library wall.

There's a frozen moment when something metallic clatters to the ground, then people swarm chattering from everywhere, pushing and shoving to see. Berkhoff is still sitting inside, staring straight ahead. Caroline Dillinger shouts out, 'Mr Berkhoff's dead!' For one horrible moment I think she must be right.

But then the car door opens. Everyone falls silent. With enormous dignity, pretending absolutely nothing is wrong, Berkhoff gets out of the driver's seat. His eye is yellowy purple and his hand is bandaged. He opens the back door and lifts out a briefcase. He turns on his heel, then, completely straight-faced, he limps off towards the staffroom, leaving his car still crunched into the wall.

Everyone watches him go, then looks at me expectantly. Clint Pocky shouts, 'Rudie made Berkhoff crash his car!'

Caroline Dillinger pushes through the crowd. She's leading a pack of Sneers. She throws her head back, points a finger at me and says, 'Ian Rude has the Evil Eye!' The crowd is suddenly in an uproar. People are pressing forward. They're all shouting and pointing at me. I don't even know what the Evil Eye is.

I say, 'What's the Evil Eye?'

Caroline Dillinger snorts. 'Like you don't *know*, Ee-yun! It's when you can make really bad things happen to people just by *looking* at them, Ee-yun!'

I'm flabbergasted. I stand in the middle of the quadrangle and shout, 'Listen, you dur-brains! I cannot hurt anyone just by looking at them!'

I look at a Year 7 girl.

She faints.

The crowd goes into uproar again.

Surely I didn't cause that? I hurry off in a panic. As I come round the corner of the library I see Ms Pewty. My stomach somersaults with shame. I veer off towards the toilets. Suddenly Bogle is in front of me. He rearranges his lips and says, 'So. My place tonight. Or I tell.'

I could deck him, but he might dob me in to Darren, Derrin and Kurt. So I spin on my heel, and bump straight into Ms Pewty. She frowns anxiously over her glasses and says, 'Oh Ian, about football training. There's an extra session tonight that you might want to attend ...' and starts rabbiting on about how wonderful it will be to meet other people who can kick like me.

I want to die with embarrassment. All I know is that I mustn't say anything about her boobs. I stare her straight in the eye. She goes on and on. I'm smiling desperately. I'm in a cold sweat telling myself, 'Don't mention the boobs. Don't say anything about the boobs.'

Now she's on to the joys of footy training. I put up a fight, saying I haven't got my sports gear. She says I don't need a shirt or shorts or any gear apart from boots which I can borrow from Lost

Property. I agree just to get rid of her, but she won't go.

I'm going cross-eyed trying to keep my eyes off her boobs. At last she winds up. She smiles. 'Just turn up. You don't need a top.'

I'm so relieved, she's going. I say, 'As long as we'll all be topless.'

I gasp, 'I mean, wearing only our boots! Oh! I didn't mean that!'

Ms Pewty says patiently, 'I think I know what you mean, Ian. And Ian?'

My face is burning. I gasp, 'Yes, Ms Pewty?'

'You haven't been doing your flexes, have you.'

'No, Ms Pewty.'

'If you do them long enough I guarantee they will calm you down. Come along. Breathe and flex. You do it.'

I pick up my imaginary suitcases and put them down again.

'Good.'

She walks off. Bogle is laughing like a drain. I turn round and swing a punch at him. I'm so little that it only wings him, but it makes me feel better. He's still laughing his head off as he crashes against some lockers and falls to the ground. I march off with my imaginary suitcases, trying not to stress.

With my mind racing, I slip into history. I apologise to Mr Chan and sit down. Amazingly, Bogle is already there in the desk next to me. He sniggers. Caroline Dillinger and the Sneers give me savage looks. Meanwhile, Clint and Cunningham grin and mime various suggestions for crippling Mr Chan. I ignore the lot of them. I need to relax. Mr Chan rattles on about ancient Egypt. It's no good. My mind keeps circling back to my problems. I need to flex.

I casually rest both my forearms on the desk. I clench my fists and start quietly flexing my biceps. It doesn't feel as if it's relaxing me, but I have to give it a chance. I get to forty. My arms are aching and I'm still tense. I'd better go for sixty. This is really hurting and I'm incredibly tense— but I am not thinking about Berkhoff! If I go for seventy-five I might lose the tension all together. Seventy-*one* ... seventy-*two* ... seventy-*three* ...

I suddenly look at Andy. He's copying me. He's got this demented grin on his face and he's flexing like a maniac.

I hiss, 'Stop it!'

He grins and keeps going. We look like we're rowing a boat together. All the tension has come back. I'd better go for a hundred.

'Stop it, Andy!'

Caroline Dillinger goes, 'What are you two doing?'

I go, 'Andy, I'll get you.'

Kristy Bogle whines, 'Stop doing that, it's weird!'

Caroline goes, 'Ee-yun! Stop it!'

Clint and Cunningham start copying us.

'Mr Chan.' It's Caroline.

Ninety-*five* ... ninety-*six* ...

'The boys are doing weird stuff and distracting us.'

Ninety-*seven* ... ninety-*eight* ...

Andy and I are rowing like crazy.

One *hundred!*

Mr Chan turns round. Andy and I have stopped, exhausted. Clint and Cunningham get sent to the Principal.

At lunchtime, I notice that every tough kid in the school is walking round chewing Teenage Energy Pills and twitching. Then I realise. They're all flexing.

Chapter 16

I observe all this through the window of the cleaner's room next to the toilets, which has become my new hiding place. I have to sit on a big metal mop bucket and there's a strong smell of toilet disinfectant, but apart from that it's okay.

I open my sandwich to find Dad's sneaked a layer of the Japanese wasabi mustard on top of the vegetarian sausage. By my calculations, our family is going to be eating this stuff for the next thirty years. I chuck away the sausage and chomp miserably on the bread. The point is, I can't go out into the schoolyard because I'll have to face the Ratbag Criminal Element. And I still haven't worked out how I'm going to fend them off—if that's possible.

I notice a tow truck arriving. It's for Berkhoff's car. Berkhoff and the man have a chat while a crowd of flexing kids gathers round to watch. The tow-truck driver attaches chains to the Barina. A big cheer goes up as the Barina starts being dragged slowly up onto the back of the tow truck. Berkhoff bellows at them to shut up and glares round with his one good eye. I feel a pang of guilt—and panic. When is this thing I've got with Berkhoff going to stop? When I kill him? I don't want to go to jail for killing some fat old maths teacher. And what exactly is the Evil Eye anyway?

At that point Berkhoff looks round, sees me—and the chain on the tow truck snaps, sending the Barina bouncing back onto the road.

I guess that's the Evil Eye.

After I've finished my lunch I nip into the library to look up the Evil Eye on the basis that it would be a good idea to understand my affliction. I type 'Evil Eye' into the computer. A Year 7 library monitor reads what I've typed, gasps in horror and scuttles off.

It's a useless exercise since the only thing on eyes is a picture book called *Your*

Wonderful Eyeball. I need to go to the public library. But I'll have to plan it carefully so I miss Darren, Derrin and Kurt. Not to mention Berkhoff and Ms Pewty and her topless football team.

As the last bell goes I'm out of the classroom like a flash. Straight into Andy Bogle. He does his weird grin and says smugly, 'You can't get away!'

'Just watch me!' I push past him.

'I'll tell!'

'Who's going to believe you?'

'They're already finding out the pills don't work. When they find out for sure, you're cactus.'

'What d'you mean?'

'I'll tell you when we've finished the cow's stomach.'

'*What?*'

'My entry for the Young Scientist competition. It's a life-size model of a ruminant's stomach, complete with four chambers. It's got to be wired up to a battery-operated tape deck so we get the right sloshing sounds. I need help with the soldering.'

He needs help with his mind. And he knows he's got me. I fall in step with him, but there's no way I'm talking to the creep. I turn my mind to the problem of how I suddenly developed the Evil Eye. I'm so engrossed that I hardly notice that we've arrived at the supermarket. Andy marches in. I follow. Now we're at the meat department in front of a display of different cuts of meat wrapped in plastic. Andy's staring at the lamb chops. He glances left at the sausages. He glances right at some pigs' liver.

He looks at me and says, 'Hmm. No kidneys.'

Then he leans over, lifts his hands and makes a pincer out of each thumb and index finger. He screws his eyes up with concentration and, as I'm standing there thinking I'm seeing things, he tweaks some chicken sausages. I blink. He does it again. Then, he lifts both hands right up in the air above his head. He looks like he's about to play a piano concerto.

Whoosh! He slaps his hands down on a leg of lamb and starts squeezing madly.

'What the hell are you doing!'

'Meat squeezing. Have a go.'

'Are you mad?'

'Squeeze that big bit of beef.'

'Stop it, you weirdo!'

'Kidneys are best. Or boneless chicken.'

127

Now he's on to the legs of pork. This can't be true. I must be having hallucinations. I cannot be trapped in a supermarket with piped music and everything completely normal except for some lunatic next to me insanely squelching the pre-packaged pork. Now he's starting on the mince!

We're going to get arrested! In ten minutes we'll be down at the police station being charged with meat-mauling. That's all I need. I crack. I suddenly feel rage welling up inside me like it did during the fight in football. I don't care whether he dobs me in or not. I give a roar and stride off down the aisle. Bogle's after me.

'I'll tell!'

'Rack off, you pervert.'

'Don't you want to hear my theories about you and Berkhoff?'

'No!'

'About magnetic force fields and allergies?'

I hesitate. Bogle's in like a flash.

'My favourite theory is pheromones.'

'Fera what?'

'Pheromones. They're very faint-smelling chemical odours given off to attract or repel other members of the same species. I think you give off pheromones that Berkhoff's allergic to.'

'You saying I stink?'

'I'm saying your pheromones might be making Berkhoff injure himself.'

I look closely at him. Any minute he's going to burst out laughing and shout 'Sucked in'. But he doesn't. This complete whacko, whose hobby is squeezing meat, seriously believes my smell makes Berkhoff crash his car. Andy sees me staring, shrugs and says, 'Fine, don't believe me. Just look in the encyclopaedia at my place.'

He is absolutely correct about pheromones being in the encyclopaedia. I call all the stuff up on the computer as Andy prepares the cow's stomach for soldering.

The stomach's quite good. If you like that sort of thing. It's done in cross-section and attached to a board. As Andy explains, cows actually have four stomachs, so the model is constructed like four odd-shaped bowls made out of papier-mâché and joined together by bits of hosepipe. The first one's got a heap of grass cuttings in it. The second and third ones have got little green balls of stuff that turn out to be handfuls of grass especially chewed by

Andy for the purpose. He reckons each one takes ages. The last stomach's got a plastic lining and holds a cupful of green runny stuff that's so disgusting I don't even want to think where it came from.

Andy reckons cows vomit up these little balls called cuds and rechew them. It really puts you off milk.

But I have to say, it's actually quite relaxing just chatting openly about my problems. Andy's chewing some grass for another cud-ball. I do one as well, to be sociable.

Andy reckons I could try some strong-smelling deodorant to smother my phero-mones. Or maybe keep a can of flyspray handy, or drench a hanky in toilet duck.

Still chewing, we solder a bit of elec-trical flex to a battery. We discuss force fields, and the chance I'm giving off an electrical charge. We hope we're wrong about that one, because it turns out the only way to stop it would be to encase myself in rubber, lead or cork. Andy suggests carrying rubber boots and a swimming cap for emergencies.

I bring up the possibility that I'm being haunted or cursed. Andy reckons I'm wrong. He's got a lot of books about the supernatural. He reckons they're mostly about ghosts out for revenge or people rising from the grave. He says he's never read one about someone who keeps accidentally assaulting their maths teacher. I ask him what he knows about exorcism. He says he'll look it up on the Net. He says, if I'm worried, I should hang some garlic round my room.

When I ask what he meant by saying that people are starting to see through the placebo effect, he says that a couple of Year 11s told the Ratbags the pills didn't work. Luckily, the Ratbags shut them up by getting everyone to laugh at them. Andy says it's an Emperor's New Clothes situation. With luck, no one else will have the nerve to criticise Teenage Energy Pills in case they get rubbished by the rest of the school.

We chew a final cud each and tape the battery to the cow's intestine. We attach it all to Andy's tape deck. He's using a tape-recording of a washing machine on the Delicates cycle for the gurgling of the cow's digestion processes. It's pretty convincing. When I announce I have to go, Andy tells me he's got a present for me. It's a container of Harpic powder, the sort of stuff you use to clean toilets. It's got a really bleachy smell to block my pheromones. Andy suggests I sprinkle a bit on my clothes tomorrow morning. I say thanks and leave.

Walking home, I realise I am the most relaxed I have been for ages. Getting a genius on my case is pretty useful, even if he does have strange habits with meat. Admittedly, I haven't worked out what to do about helping the Ratbags steal the next consignment of Teenage Energy Pills, but it's nice to think I'm not cursed.

I stop to stare at the ocean. I listen to the crashing surf. Then I notice a new sound, the roar of distant motorbikes. I glance round to see a pack of Cannibals thundering up the main street in formation, all wearing their regulation black helmet with yellow skull. Skull's leading— his black leather outfit and the bike are unmistakable. Syd's in the middle.

The formation passes me, reaches the new roundabout, arcs noisily round it, comes back up the street and stops right next to me, engines throbbing. A little Cannibal at the back of the group waves and beckons me over to his Harley.

That's funny. Who else do I know in

the Cannibals? The Cannibal who waved starts removing his helmet. He's not dressed in leathers like the others. In fact, he's a short guy dressed in jeans and a T-shirt exactly the same as ...

Wait a minute. Is that Cannibal who I think it is? Can it be? Is it?

Chapter 17

I'm clinging to Dad for dear life, but it's excellent! I'm on the back of Dad's bike and we're roaring up the freeway in formation with the rest of the Cannibals. I'm even wearing a real Cannibal crash helmet! Skull is leading, Syd is to our right, and to our left is a cheerful old guy with a Father Christmas beard and three teeth. When there's a car to overtake, we stream out in a line, then stream back in a graceful curve. When I look down at the road whizzing under the wheels it's just a blur of grey.

I can't believe how good Dad is at riding the motorbike. How come he can do something like that? When we stop for petrol I ask him. His face is glowing. He grins and says, 'Ah well, you'd be surprised at what I've got up to in my time!' And adds tenderly, 'Isn't she beautiful?'

For a surprising second I think he's talking about a woman, but then I see that he's staring, entranced, at the motorbike. It's one of those old-fashioned chopper-style ones with the handlebars raised high in the air. It belongs to Syd. Dad goes over to it. He runs his hand over its gleaming chrome curves. He turns to me and murmurs reverently, 'When I was eighteen years old, Ian, this was my dream . . .'

I can relate to that.

We go another ten kilometres up the freeway and stop for coffee in a roadside cafe called El Gringo. It has dusty Mexican hats hanging from the ceiling. There are equally dusty cactuses around the walls and the toilets are labelled Stallions and Fillies. The man who runs it is called Wozza. He's got a big Mexican-style black moustache linking his nostril hair to the hair in his ears. Dad buys me a rubbery hamburger that has a big lump of mould on the edge.

Skull buys himself a donut. He tells me he can't resist it and he's a boofhead because the way his heart is, it's pure poison. Syd puts country and western on the jukebox and gargles along with it. I learn that the Father Christmas with three teeth is called Gutsa. We talk. At my age he was a boy soprano.

Then it's time to go home. We stream back down the freeway. The bike is returned to Syd's. Dad and I agree that we keep our jaunt with the Cannibals from Mum. We giggle a bit. I'm so relaxed that I don't know myself. As we enter the shop, Mum smiles and greets us. She is reloading the shelves of dried fruit.

I'm so relaxed that at first I hardly notice Terry standing behind her. His teeth are bared, his eyes are rolling and he's waving a cordless drill.

I gasp, thinking he's about to take out Mum, but then I realise he is actually signalling. And what he's signalling is that, about a metre away from Mum's foot, sitting on its hind legs and chewing delicately on a bit of vegeburger, is the rat.

The rat is massive. Its coat gleams and its teeth are so big and white they seem to shine out of its face like something in a toothpaste commercial.

It senses something and, still chewing, looks up at us calmly. This is bizarre. It's such a peaceful scene—Mum unpacking, the rat nibbling. For a moment I think I'm seeing things, and maybe it's a puppy or something, but I'm not. Terry, Dad and I are frozen to the spot. Terry's wearing a T-shirt that reads: DON'T START PERSPIRING, LET POCKY FIX YOUR WIRING.

Then Mum becomes aware of our silence. She glances up and smiles. 'Anything wrong?'

A metre away, the rat lowers its vegeburger and, still chewing, looks over at Mum with mild curiosity.

Mum's starting to get anxious. She stares closely at Dad. 'Steve? What is it?'

Her tone scares the rat. It scuttles for the storeroom. Dad instantly swoops Mum up in his arms so she won't see. He yells, 'God you're beautiful!' and starts kissing her madly.

The rat shoots off into the storeroom. Terry and I breathe a sigh of relief. Dad finally releases Mum, who's all flushed and giggly. Dad grins triumphantly at Terry and me, then turns back to Mum and winks.

He says, 'Sorry darling, it was the way you were packing those prunes!'

Mum grins and says, 'You've always

liked this dress.' She gives a dazzling smile and goes off with a spring in her step.

When she's gone, Terry gasps, 'Struth, mate, that was a close one.'

I'm exasperated.

'Dad, why don't you just tell her?'

'Don't be dumb, son. You know the way she'd go on.'

'But it'll be worse when she finds out.'

'*If* she finds out. Look, why d'you want to worry her? We just have to modify the baits.'

At that moment, Mum comes back, clamps Dad in a passionate embrace, beams at me and starts unpacking apricots.

After dinner Dad and I sneak off to Syd's shed, where Dad's arranged a council of war to discuss the rat. Terry and Syd are both convinced that the rat is taking the bait. They suspect the bait's not working because the rat is so incredibly fit from eating health foods. They decide to increase the bait's strength.

Mick the hippy drifts into the shed. He's forgotten why he's come, but Terry remembers the reason. It's to offload a truckload of chemical-free chook manure ordered by Terry from Mick's farm in the hills. Dad, Syd and Terry help Mick unload while I hang on to Ripper, who's obsessed with the smell of Mick's plastic sandals. Discussion returns to the rat. Mick suggests that the rat might not like beer. He suggests substituting mashed pumpkin or soy milk, which he uses at his farm to great success.

The conversation comes to a close because Ripper is nearly strangling himself trying to get at the sandals, and in any case, Mick has to get back to cook dinner for his daughter from Geelong. She's a manicurist. Her speciality is hangnails.

When Mick's gone, Syd and Terry dismiss the idea of soy milk or pumpkin and decide instead to change the beer. They'll use some of Syd's home brew, which is particularly sweet. Syd brings out some for Dad to taste (I decline), and the whole thing turns into a bit of a party. Terry explains that the chook manure is part of the family's plan for Granny Pocky's birthday present. The idea is to win first prize in a funniest home video competition on TV, so Syd and Granny get a trip for two to a super-posh health resort. Their entry will involve Syd pretending to fix the roof of the shed then deliberately falling off into the pile of chook manure below.

I know the resort they mean. I've seen the TV commercial. It shows all these glamorous men and women lolling by a magnificent pool. It asks how you would feel about joining the rich and famous, and using the luxury spa. You wonder how the rich and famous would feel about being joined by Syd and Granny. Especially in the luxury spa.

As we go, Dad looks again at the Harley he borrowed, pats it, and sighs. He says, 'Well, my biking days are over, but still . . .'

That makes me a bit sad.

I say, 'Dad, why don't you get a bike?'

'Me? No way. Plenty of better things to spend cash on than a bike.'

But he stares at it longingly.

Chapter 18

Dad takes Mum for a walk along the beach while Syd and Terry add Syd's home brew and extra bait to the rat-traps. I keep watch. Troy is strapped into the highchair in the cafe while we do it. He keeps screaming and struggling to get out. I give him a bar of carob chocolate to shut him up. He tastes it, spits it out, chucks the bar on the floor and screams. I try to teach him to say 'Thank you.'

He says, 'Nick off!'

It occurs to me that this is a good chance to get myself a string of garlic from the vegetable display to ward off any evil presences in my room. There are heaps in the shop. They're tied decoratively around a tray of Mick's cauliflowers. I try to untie one, but they're attached so tightly I can't unpick the knots. I settle for a bottle of garlic salt.

Syd and Terry are finished. They hurry out the back door, then hurry back, realising they've forgotten Troy. As soon as they've gone, I go to my room to sprinkle garlic salt over the carpet. I do an extra sprinkle under the bed and near the windows. It reeks, but I suppose that's the point. I do my homework and go to bed.

I hear Dad and Mum come back. Mum's laughing. That's nice. She's been so worried about the shop I haven't heard her laugh for ages. When she comes in to say goodnight, we have a good chat. She says how well the shop is going, considering, and how she thinks that by our target time of six months we'll really have a good little business going. On impulse, I take the plunge.

'Mum . . .'

'Mm?'

'Mum, I . . .' How do you tell your mother you're turning into something out of a horror movie?

I blurt out, 'Mum, strange things are happening to me. Things I can't understand.'

Mum stares down at me, then says in this soft embarrassed voice, 'Darling, remember that book we got you about puberty?'

Oh God …

'I don't mean *that*! I mean …'

I lose my nerve as I realise there's really no way of saying what I've done to Berkhoff without it sounding as if I did it deliberately. And how can I say I've more or less agreed to help the Ratbags rob our shop? I give up. Now, of course, I've got to stop her asking questions.

I go, 'Oh, look, don't worry. I'm just … Well, my sports teacher says I've got a lot of strength and I thought I might be overdoing it with the vitamins.'

'That's just to do with growing up. You're naturally getting more muscles.' She kisses me, then chuckles. 'Wouldn't it be funny if we've accidentally discovered something to make teenagers stronger!'

I smile weakly.

Next morning I get woken up at six o'clock by the most amazing shouting and yelling from next door. I get to the window just in time to see Syd give a deafening gargle, totter and launch himself off the roof of the shed. What's he doing? I hear a round of applause from the other side of the shed, plus whistles that just have to be Terry, and I remember. The funniest home video. Do they have to do it at this time of the morning? Syd's head reappears over the roof of the shed. He climbs back up onto the roof, pretends to be hammering something, stands up, does the gargle, totters and falls off again. I yawn and decide to go for a shower. When I come back from the shower, he's still at it.

I check the garlic salt for traces of supernatural activity. It's exactly the same as it was last night. Good. I pack my bag, shake some Harpic powder over my shoes and, as an afterthought, over the armpits of my shirt. Combined with the smell of garlic salt that's got into everything, the stench is ferocious. But that's exactly what we want.

On the way to school, my guard of honour forms. As I walk in the gates, a roar goes up and people start to mob me.

'What ya gonna do today, Rudie?'

'Hey Rudie, how about getting Berkhoff with a cricket bat?'

'Poo, Rudie, you reek!'

I've had enough of this. I go, 'Right! The next one to shout anything at me gets it.'

Dead silence. I stare round at their scared faces. This is amazing—and excellent. Of course, I have absolutely no control over the Evil Eye or the pheromones or whatever it is that's running me, but they aren't to know that. The bell rings. People scuttle off, avoiding looking at me. Bogle's beside me.

'Good thinking, Ian. Keep them worried. See Berkhoff yet?'

'No.'

'He's just arrived by car with Ms Pewty.' Andy takes out a pad and pencil. 'Now, when he appears, I want you to go up really close so he can get a sniff of you.'

I lost my nerve. 'No way!'

'We have to be scientific about this.'

'Supposing I kill him!'

There's no time for me to run because at that very moment Berkhoff comes round the corner with Ms Pewty. He stops dead. I gasp. We stare at each other, terrified.

Andy whispers, 'Go up to him, you dork!' But I can't.

Ms Pewty smiles, blinks, and sucks in some air. She says, 'Hi Ian!' and nudges Berkhoff, who, like me, is also frozen to the spot. She takes his arm and yanks at it. Still staring at me, he starts to walk off with her.

I'm holding my breath. Nothing has happened to him. They keep walking. Still nothing has happened. Have I got the answer? Can I dare to hope? Berkhoff and Ms Pewty disappear inside the science building.

I let out a gasp of triumph.

Yes!

I dance about, punching the air. It's solved! We've done it. The answer is pheromones and Andy solved it. But all Andy does is scribble something in a notebook.

He says cautiously, 'We can't tell for sure. It'll be three days before I'm fully convinced.'

Well, *I'm* fully convinced. I walk into geography in a happy dream. People are urging me to zap Mrs Mills so all her buttons fly off. But I just smile. Cunningham wheezes that the price of Teenage Energy Pills has rocketed and that everything that goes wrong in the school is being blamed on me and my Evil Eye. But I don't care. Harpic and garlic will keep me safe.

At recess I lock myself in the dunny and give my armpits and chest another sprinkle of Harpic. I take a deep sniff and nearly choke from the fumes. But so what? They represent freedom.

The day passes in a fug of Harpic fumes and happiness. I find out I'm booked in with the counsellor, who's a skinny old man with a beard. He spends the entire interview watching me like a hawk and nervously gripping the arms of his chair. He also sniffs a lot, which I dismiss as a nervous twitch until I uncross my arms and get an overpowering whiff of sweat, Harpic and garlic, and realise that what he's sniffing is me.

He starts asking questions about my home life, which he clearly expects to be like the Addams Family. He tells me I need to relax and gives me two brochures. One is on personal hygiene, the other is called 'Proud to be me'. It advises you not to worry about being broke, unattractive and hated. He says I have to come back next week. When I say I have camp next week, he brightens. He says in that case it will have to be the week after—when he's not here. I'll be seeing a very nice lady called Mrs Sitwell. She has, he says, a lot of experience with people like me.

When I get back to class, Andy tells me

the word is that Darren and Derrin are at war over the profits from Teenage Energy Pills. This is good. It will keep everyone's mind off the fact that the pills are useless. Also, the word is that Ms Pewty and Berkhoff are an item. She must pity him. And let's face it, there's a lot to pity.

After school we go to the supermarket. Rump steak is on special, so Andy's come in for a squeeze. I watch. Actually, watching him, meat-squeezing seems strangely attractive. I find myself eyeing some chicken fillets, and have to exercise serious restraint to stop myself going for a tweak.

I'm happy.

I get back to the shop in a party mood. Which is just as well, because a party mood has overtaken our shop. The footpath outside is jammed with motorbikes and the café is packed with Cannibals noisily hoeing into the health foods. Skull's nowhere to be seen, but Syd's behind the counter, gargling out orders to Gutsa, the one who looks like Father Christmas. Syd's gargles are even louder than usual because he has to shout over the noise of Gutsa putting oranges through the electric juicer. Gutsa's tucked his Santa beard into his T-shirt, whether

148

for hygiene or to stop it getting trapped in the juicer I don't know.

Meanwhile, Mum and Dad are having a quarrel by the lentils. Dad says customers are customers and we're making a fortune. Mum says these particular customers are louts. Dad says they're not. At that moment a prissy old lady with tree-trunk legs walks past outside. Gutsa yells out, 'Give us a kiss, darlin'!', roars with laughter, and burps.

Then, through the din, Mum, Dad and I become aware of a noise like an approaching swarm of bees. It's three huge motorbikes. In fact, it's Skull and two mates roaring up in formation and stopping six centimetres away from our plate glass window. They give their bikes one final, throaty rev, remove their helmets and enter. Skull's wearing a bandanna. The two newcomers beam through broken noses and missing teeth.

The effect on the other Cannibals is amazing. They cheer and whoop in welcome. Skull sees Mum, plants a kiss on her cheek and yells proudly, 'Introducing, the famous Dirk and Lily!' Dropping his voice, he murmurs, 'Don't worry. They've brought their medication.'

Mum gives a strangled gasp and storms off. Dad's a bit taken aback himself, but soon rallies. He cheerfully tells Lily (who's a man) that smoking is not allowed. Lily stubs his cigarette out in one of the hanging baskets. He jokes that before he'd been to counselling, a remark like that would have got Dad a punch in the throat.

We all laugh wildly.

The Cannibals crowd round Dirk and Lily. Syd arrives with oat bran muffins and freshly squeezed orange juice. I learn that Dirk and Lily are legendary bikers. Dirk tells me how the scar on his forehead came from going headfirst through the window of a dry-cleaner's in Oodnadatta, whereas the one on his cheek was from a simple knife fight. Lily asks if Dad has any natural tranquillising pills. Dad suggests St John's Wort. There's some confusion about whether we're selling warts once attached to St John, and Gutsa gets quite emotional about his days as a boy soprano. He says his 'Silent Night' was awesome. Lily requests 'Away in a Manger'. The whole café joins in. Dad winks at me as if to say, 'See? Harmless after all.'

He says, 'Go and get Mum.'

I find her packing a suitcase.

Chapter 19

For a terrible moment I think Mum's
walking out on us. In fact, she's actually
packing to go to the Healthy Life Convention in Melbourne tomorrow. This is an
annual convention and exhibition where
health shop owners and people who like
health foods get to check out all the new
products. Mum is setting up a stand
showing our Rude Health Teenage Energy
Pills and, of course, the Rude Health vegeburger. She's driving to Melbourne tomorrow morning and staying for a week.

I feel a wave of relief because I'd completely forgotten about the convention. I
relax again. That's until she turns to me
and says, 'Ian, I'm about to go down to
the shop and get rid of those terrible
bikies. While I'm away I'm relying on you

to ring me if your father lets any of them anywhere near the shop.'

'But Mum!'

'No buts. You ring me. And Ian. Have a shower.'

Before I can protest, she strides off downstairs. Almost instantly there's a deafening roar as forty or so motorcycles go streaming off down the main street. Ah well, nothing can spoil my good mood, not even being made chief dobber. I go down to make myself a milkshake. Syd is just leaving through our kitchen.

He winks, grins and gargles, 'Aaaaah, lova womana spirit, a cheeky begga, aaaah!'

Despite what Mum says, I don't shower before bed and, to be on the safe side, I give my room an extra sprinkle of garlic salt. The next morning it's undisturbed. I glow with happiness and smile at the new day. But I'm still playing it safe. I don't shower and I give my clothes a good dusting with Harpic. I reek and I'm starting to itch a bit but I can live with it.

When I come downstairs, Mum and Dad are packing the car with refrigerated boxes of vegeburgers ready for the convention. I help, happily singing to myself.

Mum has to find space for a special display packed full of Teenage Energy Pills. I'm a bit rattled by the sight. If the Ratbags had known about these there would have been a riot. Still, they didn't, so what do I care? I start singing again. But, just in case the word gets out, I load them as quickly as possible.

Finally, the car is packed. Mum kisses us both, tells me I really must have a shower and reminds me to get all my stuff ready for next week's camp. As Dad and I are standing on the pavement, ready to wave her off, she rolls down her window and calls out, 'Don't forget to water the hanging baskets! And Ian …' She raises her eyebrows and stares at me knowingly. This is her way of reminding me I am dobber-in-chief. I can handle it. In fact, at the moment I can handle anything.

As Dad and I wave Mum off, I feel a surge of well-being. Dad sniffs and asks if I can smell something weird. I shake my head innocently.

I set off for school. Again, Berkhoff and I face each other, and again nothing happens. Andy makes a note on his pad. Life is good. I walk into maths. Berkhoff walks into maths. He takes a long look at me through narrowed eyes. He's staring at me for ages. I feel a flash of panic. Why is he glaring at me like that?

He suddenly snaps, 'How do we know that two triangles are congruent, Ian Rude!'

'Er . . . er . . .'

He jams his face so near to mine I get a close-up of his whiskers.

'Well, come on, Mr Rude! Pythagoras' theorem?'

'The area of the hypotenuse . . . I mean, the area of the square on the hypotenuse . . .'

'Not fast enough, that should be second nature! A car travelling at sixty kilometres an hour has two stops of one minute and three minutes respectively and reaches its destination in two hours fifty-one minutes. How long is the journey?'

'Er . . . er . . .'

He bellows, 'Right! Out here in the Castle!'

I leap up, drop my book, pick it up, drop my pencil.

'Very funny, Mr Class Clown. Now get out here!'

Before I even sit down in the Castle, he's off again, rattling questions at the speed of an automatic rifle, chucking chalk, banging on the desk, calling me sarcastic names. Even the answers I know I forget. It's terrible. The revenge of Berkhoff. He's working himself up into a frenzy. And it's not only me that's getting it. He's shocking to everyone. And it's not like the old days when he did the gallop and you could have a good laugh. He's really lost it.

You feel he could kill someone.

By the end of class, twenty-two people are on detention, the Castle has swollen to fifteen desks and Berkhoff's setting us practically the whole textbook as tonight's homework.

I go home in shock, ignoring Andy's offer to chew a few more cuds and the shouts of the angry mob telling me I stink and asking why I don't just cripple Berkhoff now and get it over with. As I walk into our garden, I hear Dad's cheerful voice. 'G'day, Ian. What do you think of this?'

I turn round. He's dressed in full leathers and sitting astride the Harley.

Dad's a Cannibal.

I'm speechless. I sink down on the back steps as Dad cheerfully explains how

155

the leather outfit came second-hand from Gutsa, who's too fat for it and gave it to Dad in return for some accountancy advice about his carpet repair business, which is called Pile Busters. Dad's pleased because the shop was never empty of Cannibals today. He's made heaps of money with a new peach smoothie called a Petrol Head. He's also invented a Vegeburger-with-the-Lot called The Harley, and a cheese and avocado melt called Full Throttle.

I just look at him. He's completely relaxed. Dad says he knows I'm worried about Mum's ban on bikers, but I'm not to be concerned because we're making a fortune. Bikers are coming from miles around. Wozza is thinking of closing El Gringo, and Skull has negotiated a list of rules for biker attendance at our place. These include no credit, no smoking and no gang warfare within a hundred metres of the shop.

He adds that I'm not to be surprised to find Terry laying rat baits in the house because the rat was in our living room today. This is nothing to worry about because the rat, while still alive, is definitely sick-looking. I'm to shower, make myself a drink and a snack while he goes for a quick burn on the chopper. He adds that Mick is staying to dinner. In fact, Mick's staying. He's using our spare room for a few days because the solar panels have fallen off his hut.

Mum rings. She says, 'Everything okay at the shop?'

I pause. I scratch my itching armpit.

'Yes, Mum.'

She says, 'Oh, I forgot. The Teenage Energy Pills. Can you tell Dad a new consignment's arriving on Friday?'

Chapter 20

The week passes in a blur of Cannibals partying, Berkhoff bellowing, people at school demanding homicide and, last but not least, a constant low-level itch from the Harpic. I daren't wash it off in case I injure Berkhoff (not that I don't want to). On top of everything else I also have to worry about the new consignment of Teenage Energy Pills arriving on Friday. If they get to the shelves before the Ratbags get them, I'll be cactus. As it is, the Ratbags are seriously resentful that I'm not maiming Berkhoff because Berkhoff, who seems set on punishing the entire universe, is threatening to suspend them for making fart noises every time he walks past.

The only good news is that the rat

is missing suspected dead in Syd's hydrangeas. And the only relaxation I have is helping Andy with the cow's stomach —in return for him assisting me with the crippling amounts of maths homework Berkhoff is giving everyone. We chew cuds and endlessly discuss solutions to my problems.

Each night, Dad cooks a dinner incorporating dollops of the Japanese wasabi. Each night Mick gets out his guitar and plays Bob Dylan hits until one o'clock in the morning, when he switches to Leonard Cohen. Sometimes Dad joins in.

Dad's wildly happy—so happy he believes my story that I'm showering every day and the extraordinary pong is caused purely by an afternoon jog. He spends a lot of time whizzing about on the Harley, which Syd is loaning him in return for tax advice on his motorbike business. I haven't got the heart to bring him down to earth. I don't know what Mum will say about it.

Well, I do. And it won't be complimentary.

It worries me the most of anything. Mum hates bikes and Cannibals. Dad loves them. How can they resolve that?

I'm torn between the two of them. I can see Mum's point about the Cannibals being off-putting and dangerous. But Dad's right that they're bringing money into the shop. What's more (and I feel really disloyal to Mum saying this), the Cannibals are *fun*, heaps more than customers like the psycho vicar or the weird dentist woman or that old biddy with her bottle of gallstones.

And I know they're dangerous. They're dangerous and fun, just like their motorbikes. And here's another thing. Dad's not the only one in the family to be hooked on Harleys. Now I am as well, and I don't know how I'm going to hide it from Mum.

Meanwhile, it's Friday, the day before she's back, so I don't have to worry about that one. Anyway, I've got enough to worry about. Today's the arrival date of the new consignment of Teenage Energy Pills. I have to intercept delivery so the Ratbags won't know they're here and raid the shop. For the first time in my life I'm illegally taking the day off school. I reckon my life's worth it.

I go down to open the shop early. Now that our only customers are Cannibals, we don't usually open until ten. I'm planning to hide the Teenage Energy Pills at the back of the storeroom until I can work out what to do with them. The storeroom reeks because Syd accidentally dropped a rat trap full of home brew.

Not that I can talk.

I wait until nine o'clock. Then it's ten, and Syd appears for some cat's claw, followed by Skull, Gutsa and Lily, who's after St John's Wort. It's eleven, the place is packed, and Dad's hard at work on the Full Throttles while I do Petrol Heads non-stop. Dad seems to have forgotten I'm supposed to be at school. Syd's behind the counter helping. He's brought in his tape deck and we've got country and western going full blast.

Still no Teenage Energy Pills. It's lunchtime, and still no Teenage Energy Pills. Instead, a visit from twelve bikers from the Warrabadanga Pirates, a highly respected gang. The Cannibals toast them with strawberry Petrol Heads. The Pirates return the toast with freshly squeezed orange juice. Gutsa launches into 'Amazing Grace'. We all join in. Gutsa does 'Ave Maria' and 'Jerusalem'. Just as he starts a request for 'The

Little Drummer Boy', I hear a voice say, 'What on earth . . .' I turn around.

It's Mum.

Dad sees her and gasps in horror. He beams nervously and goes across to welcome her in. She stares daggers at him, says, 'I think we need to talk,' and leads him off to the kitchen.

Syd and I look at each other.

Syd fakes a jovial face and goes, 'Aaaah, closing up a shoppa lazy beggas, go ado some worka, aaah!'

The Cannibals take the hint and start leaving. Meanwhile, I've dashed to the kitchen door. I peek in. Mum and Dad are arguing in fierce whispers. She's telling him the Cannibals are vandals and thugs and he's saying they're not, they're great and we're making a pile of money out of them. She's saying how could he deliberately go against her wishes and he's saying he's got wishes too and what's so wrong about people who ride bikes, as a matter of fact, he's started to ride again. She says, 'Oh Steve, how could you?' He says, 'Because the shop isn't going to go to rack and ruin just because I take an hour off!' and he bangs his fist against the pantry door so it swings open to show, sitting on

162

its hind legs swaying, the rat, dead drunk.

Dad yells and lunges at it. The rat panics, careers crazily round the kitchen and shoots out into the shop. Two seconds later, it's shooting back in again, with Syd in hot pursuit. Syd and Dad collide. Mum and Syd collide. The rat runs straight up the kitchen wall and scuttles wildly along the top of the cupboards. Mick comes in the back door to tell us the delivery of Teenage Energy Pills has arrived. There's so much yelling he freezes in the doorway, amazed. The rat sees its chance. It zips to the end of the cupboard nearest the back door, hurls itself into mid-air, clears Mick's shoulder by ten centimetres and lands somewhere out in the back yard. We all rush to the back door. We're just in time to see the rat disappearing over the fence next to the lane.

There's a moment of silence, then Mick nods his head thoughtfully and says, 'Whoa ... speeding rat ...'

Mum explodes. She yells at Dad, sees me, sniffs, drags me off to have a shower, sends me back for another shower (because she can smell that I didn't use soap so I wouldn't set off my pheromones) and says that if I come out smelling again she will personally take to me with the garden hose and a scrubbing brush. She will do the same if I ever skip school again—and don't start acting like a Cannibal in this house because it is simply not allowed.

She tells Dad to put the Teenage Energy Pills on display in the window while she runs me to school.

He says, 'You could be civil.'

She says, 'You could be reliable.'

I get into the car.

As we drive, Mum keeps up a non-stop monologue about how terrible the Cannibals are and how we're probably infested with rats and how disappointed she is I didn't ring her. The underlying message is fury with Dad. I sigh. This is horrible. What's more, I think all the soap I've had to use has made my armpits sore and slightly worsened the itch.

Mum raves on about how our business will be ruined if the town discovers we have vermin. Meanwhile, I've decided that I'll reapply the Harpic and garlic salt as soon as she's left. It's double maths this afternoon, so I'm taking no chances.

As soon as Mum's dropped me off, I whip the Harpic powder and garlic salt from my bag and give my armpits and chest a good sprinkle. I take off my shoes and sprinkle a heap inside. For good measure I chuck some down my back.

Excellent.

I let out a contented sigh.

A second later, I feel a burning sensation in my armpits. It's followed by a fierce itch. The same thing's happening to my chest, now to my feet and back. I'm one enormous, burning itch. I don't know where to scratch first. I go for my armpits. I pull off my shoes and socks and start scratching my feet. My feet are bright red all the way up to the ankle. It looks as if I'm wearing red socks.

But I can't think about that because my armpits are driving me crazy. Scraping my feet against the ragged concrete edge of a step, I rip off my shirt and start scratching my armpits. Scratching only makes it worse. What can I do? I look round frantically. I can wash it off in the drinking fountain!

A Year 7 boy is having a drink. I yell, 'Out of the way,' and tear him aside. People are screaming and shouting. A huge crowd has formed. I direct the spray on my left armpit, while wiping my feet on the concrete base like it's a doormat. Neither thing works. It's hopeless.

I run madly towards the toilets, scratching both armpits like a demented chimp. The Year 9 girls' basketball team is standing outside. They all scream. I crash through the middle of them and make it inside. I skid on the wet floor and nearly collide with two kids washing their hands. Cursing and sobbing, I push them aside, stick my right foot into a wash basin and turn the cold tap on full blast.

For two seconds there's relief. Then the itching comes raging back.

I howl in despair. I take out my right foot and plunge in my left. Then I take that out and try to submerge each armpit. Meanwhile, I'm splashing my chest.

Andy's come along to tell me off.

'Where were you this morning? You were supposed to help me bring in the cow's stomach!'

'Scratch my armpit.'

'Scratch your own bloody armpit.'

A crowd of boys is pressing into the toilets to watch.

I go, 'Twenty cents to anyone who'll scratch my armpit.'

People shout, 'Ya pervert!'

I see the cleaner's left a scrubbing brush in a corner. With one foot still in the wash basin, I hop around, grab it and start scrubbing my chest. The relief ... I do my armpits.

Wonderful!

I'm hopping on one leg in a huge puddle of water. My other foot is in the wash basin. I'm bare except for my shorts. I'm scouring my armpits with a scrubbing brush and groaning in ecstasy.

It's at this point Berkhoff bursts through the crowd, does his Tyrannosaurus roar and yells, 'Okay, Rude, hand over that marijuana.'

Chapter 21

It was Caroline Dillinger. She told Berkhoff that Andy and I were chewing grass
while boasting about disembowelling a
cow. The whole staffroom came out for
the kill—and witnessed me running half-
dressed around the quadrangle, swearing,
scraping my feet and spraying my armpits
in the drinking fountain.

Half the school thinks I'm on hard
drugs. The other half thinks I'm possessed.
No one believes I'm on Harpic.

Now Andy and I are in the Principal's
room with Berkhoff, Ms Pewty and Mrs
Mitchell, the Acting Principal. I'm coated
in calamine lotion and Berkhoff's having
a ball. He's been at me and Andy so long
Mrs Mitchell's secretary's brought him
and the others tea. He's really showing off.

He's striding up and down with his arms behind his back like a lawyer in the movies. He's got one of Andy's cuds.

He shoves his face into mine and bellows, 'Admit you were eating marijuana.'

My armpits are starting to itch again. I whisper, 'I wasn't, sir.'

'Then what *were* you doing?'

I give up, and whisper, 'I don't know.'

He bellows, 'You don't know! You don't know! Well, perhaps you can explain why you were running around the quadrangle half-naked, gibbering like a monkey and dangling your armpits in the bubbler, Mr Rude.'

He holds out one of Andy's cuds.

'What is this?'

'Grass, sir . . .'

'Ha! We have it. A confession!'

I interrupt, 'No, *grass*! The stuff cows eat.'

'Don't raise your voice to me. I'm getting sick of you, Rude. I knew from the moment you set foot in this school you were going to be trouble. Ms Pewty has given you chances. I've given you chances, but you . . .'

He stops, spins on his heel and looks

at Ms Pewty and Mrs Mitchell just to see what a great impression he's making.

'What do you do? You have some kind of terrible drug overdose in the school grounds. You hallucinate in front of the fountain. You burst into the school toilets and offer money to people to scratch your armpits. Now, you twisted, depraved, nasty delinquent, before we call in your parents, what caused this attack?'

I look at his big demented face. Now he's picking up his cup of tea. All that bellowing has given him a thirst. I think of all the trouble I've gone to, to stop myself from hurting him. I think of how much I've worried about him. I think how I can never expect to be happy at this school as long as he's here.

I can feel the itching coming back. And with it, I feel my rage rising. I think, 'I wish you were dead, Berkhoff.'

Berkhoff's gulping down his tea. His eye catches mine. He stares back. Then he chokes and coughs. Suddenly he's coughing and spluttering and staggering around the room. Tears are rolling down his face. Mrs Mitchell slaps him on the back. Ms Pewty gives him a slap.

Oh no, I've killed him!

Mrs Mitchell and Ms Pewty are shouting. Berkhoff's looking at me out of desperate bloodshot eyes.

Please don't die!

Berkhoff gags, reels, gasps, goes red as a beetroot. But he doesn't die.

It might have been better if he had. Because, in all the fuss, he forgets to suspend me, or even to ring my parents. But he's already got the Ratbags suspended. And the Ratbags are furious with me in any case because the new consignment of Teenage Energy Pills is at the centre of our window display and can't realistically be hijacked.

A message arrives for me via Clint and Cunningham. It's a note.

It reads: 'Last chance, runt. Get rid of Berkhoff.'

They give it to me as I'm walking along the beach with Andy, trying to work out what set off my powers again and what I can possibly do to fix things between Mum and Dad. We don't have answers to either. Now, on top of everything else, I'm supposed to murder Berkhoff, or at least get him to leave the school.

Andy's all for the latter. Personally, I

think Berkhoff's having such a good time monstering everyone at school that the only way to get him out of the place would be feet first. Andy disagrees. He says we should make a move during our geography camp, which starts tomorrow. He reckons we could force Berkhoff to leave by getting him to make a total fool of himself in front of all the other teachers. I say Berkhoff's doing a pretty good job of that all on his own. And anyway, he's got Ms Pewty to stay for.

Maybe the one to leave town should be me. If I didn't have Mum and Dad to worry about, I would. I'd run away tomorrow. Andy points out that since we're going to camp tomorrow (which the Ratbags aren't attending), I at least have two days' grace before they get me. We watch the surf miserably.

I get home to find Mum and Dad arguing in the kitchen, Granny Pocky, Syd and Terry scrubbing the storeroom from top to bottom, and Mick wandering anxiously about with some boxes of grapefruit. He assures me that it's good Mum's giving vent. There's not a Cannibal in sight. In fact, the shop is completely empty. I put myself on duty behind the counter. Everywhere I move I leave a trail of pink powder from the dried calamine. From the time I arrive until closing time we don't have a single customer.

Mum and Dad shut up the shop in stony silence. We eat dinner in stony silence. I go up to my bedroom. It's gleaming and meticulously tidy with not a speck of garlic salt in sight. Mum's obviously been furious all afternoon. I get my camp stuff together, including a bottle of calamine lotion and a tube of anti-itch cream. The list says I'll need a torch and batteries for the bivouac, so I slip out to the supermarket. I get back to see Dad whizzing off on the Harley in his Cannibal outfit. Mum's in the kitchen, grimly cleaning out the cutlery drawer.

She says, 'Well, Ian, I've told your father. It's the Cannibals or us.'

So that's it. The thing I didn't dare to think about. My parents are splitting up.

I go to bed miserable. I wake up worse. The sheets are full of pink dust from the calamine. I stare at the ceiling and assess my situation. Number one, my powers are back. Number two, the Ratbags will beat me up unless I get rid of Berkhoff. Number three, I still itch. Number four, and by far the worst of everything, is that my parents are separating and there's not a thing I can do.

I feel a surge of irritation at myself. What a wuss! There must be *something* I can do. I can't just lay back and let my parents split up because I'm too taken up with problems at school.

They need me.

I sit up in bed. That's it, my parents need me. I'm the only one who can bring them together again. How I'll do it I don't know. What I *do* know is that I have to give it my best shot. I have to clear up my school problems so I'm free to concentrate on the family. If I can just get rid of Berkhoff my school problems will end. There'll be no more Berkhoff to get me into trouble and people will respect me for getting rid of him. I'll still have the Placebo Effect to worry about, but I'll worry about that one later.

I can do it at camp, as Andy suggested. I'll have to be quick. Camp's only two days, so it's very little time to get rid of Berkhoff but a lot of time for things to worsen between Mum and Dad.

That's my answer. I get up. I shower. I apply the anti-itch cream.

Two days to get rid of Berkhoff.

Chapter 22

At breakfast Mum and Dad are still not talking. I try to say things that will force them to speak to each other. It doesn't work. We drive to the bus in silence. It's even worse than the silence of last night, if that's possible. This rattles me a bit, but I'm determined not to let it put me off my plan. Get Berkhoff out of town. Get my parents back together.

There's not a minute to be wasted. We arrive just as the bus is pulling in. As soon as I possibly can, I get rid of Mum and Dad and take Andy aside. He reckons I'm doing the right thing. This is confirmed by Clint and Cunningham, who come up, give me a wedgie and say that if I don't get Berkhoff at camp I'm cactus. A crowd gathers to agree.

Andy and I get in the bus and start racking our brains for incidents that would embarrass Berkhoff so much he'll leave the school. We decide we need a whole series of things. The bivouac sounds like promising material. Also, we know there'll be water sports at camp, so there's a good chance we can do something like get him in a rowing boat and take away the oars. Now my pheromones are back in action, luck should be on our side.

The big problem, of course, is Ms Pewty. She really likes him. And Berkhoff would be mad to walk away from a woman who's interested in him. There can't have been many in his life. In fact, it's amazing enough there's even been one. We need to put her off him—and him off her. But how?

Out the window we can see Berkhoff stomping about in a baseball cap and a brand new purple ski jacket. He's trying to impress Ms Pewty. He looks like a giant blackcurrant on legs.

He gets on the bus and starts ticking us all off the list. Then, because he wants to make sure Ms Pewty sits next to him, he calls out, 'Anyone seen Ms Pewty?' Out of nowhere I get a brainwave. Quick as a flash, I say, 'She's ringing her husband.'

Berkhoff freezes. Andy stares at me in amazed delight. I feel a mixture of guilt and terror in case Berkhoff sees through the lie. But he doesn't. He's crushed. I've put him off Ms Pewty! And it gets better. Berkhoff gets off the bus and two seconds later Ms Pewty gets on, looking for him. She calls out, 'Is Mr Berkhoff about?' Andy yells out, 'He's ringing his wife!'

She's crushed as well! Andy and I can't believe our luck. We feel a bit guilty about deceiving someone as nice as Ms Pewty, but we figure she'll thank us in years to come.

The bus engine starts up. Ms Pewty and Berkhoff sit at different ends of the bus. Berkhoff is being vicious to everyone.

Excellent.

The bus roars loudly along the main road with the whole of Year 8 roaring loudly along inside. Cunningham is trying to beat his record for swallowing three packets of corn chips in one mouthful. Andy is reading a Japanese dictionary. We stop at traffic lights outside the church. The psycho vicar looms up from behind a sign reading LAY DOWN YOUR BURDEN and shakes his fist at me. Caroline Dillinger goes, 'Oh, Mr Berkhoff, Ian Rude's annoying a vicar.'

I tell her to nick off.

The bus trip takes about three hours (not counting time for Cunningham to be sick next to a statue of two pioneers) and finishes halfway up a range of mountains in the middle of nowhere. This place is called Beringa. It consists of a collection of big and little log cabins in a clearing surrounded by tree-covered mountains. There's a river with canoes and sailboards. There's an old four-wheel drive and an older ute. That's about it.

The man who greets us says he and his wife are the only people for a hundred k's and before he's letting us dump our gear we have to spend a moment listening to the silence. We stand there listening. Clint Pocky does an armfart and gets told off. We have to start again.

I spend my moment of silence checking out the possibilities for getting Berkhoff. Andy does the same. He nods towards something. I look. Cables. They're going down our hill and across the valley to the other side. I follow them back to where they start. I recognise them as part of a flying fox, one of those things where you sit on a seat (or if you're big, in a harness like a giant nappy), then someone gives you a shove and you whiz off down the line. So?

Andy grins and whispers, 'Physics.'

I'm dying to find out what he's on about, but there's no chance. The man who runs the camp insists on silence while he tells us the rules of the place: no littering, no getting lost and watch out for poisonous snakes. Berkhoff takes over with another lot of rules. Finally, Ms Pewty blows her whistle, frowns, ignores Berkhoff and tells us to dump our gear outside the dining hall and assemble at the flying fox up the hill.

As we head for the dining hall, Andy explains. We have to get Berkhoff to have a go on the flying fox. The point is, for a normal-sized person, it would just be a pleasant, leisurely ride. But, according to Andy, the laws of physics mean that if someone of Berkhoff's huge weight gets into the giant nappy, they go whizzing down at incredible speed. What's more, they go at such a rate that when they hit the end of the run the impact knackers them.

In other words, we get Berkhoff to give himself a giant wedgie.

We fall about laughing. Clint and Cunningham come up and ask what we're laughing about. They add it'd better be about getting Berkhoff or they'll thump us. We tell them. They also fall about laughing. In fact, the idea of Berkhoff hurtling down the flying fox at a hundred k's an hour gets Cunningham laughing so much he has to have three sucks on his Ventolin puffer. The minute he can breathe, he immediately packs up again laughing.

People gather to find out what the joke is. Clint tells about fifteen people, warning them that one word to Caroline Dillinger and they're dead meat. They fall about as well. Nobody can wait. We hurry up to the top of the flying fox. As soon as Berkhoff arrives with Ms Pewty and Mr Chan, people start shouting, 'Have a go on the flying fox, Mr Berkhoff. It's really cool, sir. You'll love it, Mr Berkhoff.'

Berkhoff blasts irritably on his whistle.

'Shut up the lot of you. Now. Ms Pewty will demonstrate how to use the flying fox. Anyone who doesn't listen is on detention. Ms Pewty?'

Ms Pewty is refusing to look at him. She sucks air through her teeth and walks over to the flying fox. She holds up the seat and goes on about what you do. Nobody's paying attention. We're all whispering and giggling and staring at Berkhoff. He's standing there, scowling at Ms Pewty and looking at his watch.

As soon as Ms Pewty finishes, people are back on at Berkhoff to have first go. He refuses. So Mr Chan, who thinks we're all just getting into the jolly spirit of camp life, goes all jovial and says *he'll* have a go. Ms Pewty goes all jolly as well. She jokes about with him as she helps him into the big nappy. Berkhoff is watching. You can see he's jealous.

Ms Pewty gives Mr Chan a shove. He shouts, 'Geronimo!' and goes speeding off. Everyone cheers, then immediately starts in again on Berkhoff.

'Oh please, Mr Berkoff.'

'Give it a go, Mr Berkhoff.'

'Be a sport, Mr Berkhoff.'

Ms Pewty suddenly starts as well, but her voice has an edge to it.

She says, challengingly, 'Yes, why don't you?'

We all hold our breath. Berkhoff looks at her. They're really annoyed with each other. Then Berkhoff grunts irritably and says, really miffed, 'Right, Ms Pewty, I will.'

Yes!

Andy and I are ecstatic. People are jumping in circles, cheering. Berkhoff ambles sulkily over towards the harness. I move as close to him as possible in case my pheromones can add to the disaster. Ms Pewty avoids his eyes and starts hauling back the nappy in preparation. Andy gives me a thumbs up. This is wonderful. A giant wedgie in front of Ms Pewty! It couldn't be better. I'm so anxious for it to happen I give Ms Pewty a hand with the hauling. I give an enormous yank.

And the nappy jams.

Chapter 23

It's stuck halfway along the cable. I can't believe it. Ms Pewty and I pull and yank at the cable. Then Berkhoff joins in, followed by Clint, Cunningham and half of the class. Cunningham's nearly crying at the thought of Berkhoff not getting the giant wedgie. Ms Pewty keeps suggesting we play volleyball instead. No-one listens. We're all frantically swinging and tugging on the cable because we know there'll never be anything half as funny in our entire lives as Berkhoff getting the giant wedgie. Finally, the man who runs the place comes up and tells us to stop. The flying fox is officially out of order. He says he's set up the net for volleyball.

It takes two seconds for the ball to whack me on the back of the head. It's

Cunningham. He reckons I jammed the nappy on purpose.

Nothing could be further from the truth, which is that I'm desperate. We've lost our best chance to humiliate Berkhoff, time is ticking away and Berkhoff is nowhere to be seen.

Volleyball finishes. Water sports are about to start and there's still no sign of Berkhoff. Andy and I confer. Until we know what sport Berkhoff is going to be supervising, we can't plan a thing.

We get to the lake and there's still no sign of him. Ms Pewty is already organising the sailboarding. Then we see him. He's walking down the hill towards us. More accurately, a canoe with black hairy legs is walking down the hill towards us. Berkhoff's inside, carrying it. He's wearing enormous Hawaiian board shorts and an orange life jacket.

He wades out into the lake, swings the canoe off his head and into the water and bellows for silence. He says, 'Right. Everyone interested in canoeing, over here. I will be demonstrating.'

Andy and I exchange a look. While Berkhoff's rabbiting on, we go through all the possibilities, from taking his paddle to puncturing the canoe. We decide to capsize him in front of Ms Pewty for maximum possible embarrassment. We can't work out how to do it without being seen, but just then Clint and Cunningham come up ready for some general menacing. We rope them in to help.

The plan is simple. I will get a canoe. Andy will position himself near Ms Pewty at the sailboarding and Clint and Cunningham will go swimming. We'll all behave normally for a few minutes, at which time I will casually paddle up behind Berkhoff and try to project dangerous pheromones. At a given sign, Clint will pretend to be drowning. When Berkhoff goes across for the rescue, Clint will grab his paddle and pull hard, pretending to be panicking. Meanwhile, I will be paddling as near to Berkhoff as possible so my bow-wave gets his canoe rocking crazily and taking in water. Cunningham will assist me by deliberately splashing water into the back of Berkhoff's canoe.

With all of us working on it like this, Berkhoff will have to caspize. And Andy will be there to make sure Ms Pewty and Mr Chan witness the whole embarrassing event.

Everyone agrees. Clint and Cunningham immediately tell a heap of other people. They're all giggling and watching. We wait for Berkhoff to launch his canoe and paddle out onto the lake. Then I get into a canoe, Clint and Cunningham swim out to the middle of the lake, and Andy stands right next to Ms Pewty. By now, Berkhoff is paddling up and down, happily bossing everyone.

Here goes. I take a deep breath, paddle up behind Berkhoff and concentrate fiercely on his fat back. I'm willing terrible things to happen to him. I get closer and closer. Just as I'm about a metre away from him, I signal Clint.

He shouts, 'Help! Help! I've got cramp. Mr Berkhoff!'

Berkhoff paddles desperately towards Clint, with me paddling desperately behind Berkhoff.

Berkhoff sticks out his paddle and shouts, 'Grab hold of this!'

Clint yanks on it for all he's worth. Meantime, I open my eyes wide and stare fiercely at Berkhoff's fat orange back while Andy yells, 'Ms Pewty, look at Mr Berkhoff!'

But Berkhoff doesn't capsize. The next

thing I see is a huge amount of splashing and Clint being hauled high out of the water on the end of Berkhoff's paddle. I can't believe it. Berkhoff's rescued him. As my mouth drops open in surprise, the waves made by all the splashing hit my canoe. I've only got a moment to yell out before the canoe capsizes—right on top of Cunningham.

Berkhoff rescues me, then Cunningham, who's concussed. He drags us all out to the beach, where all the teachers congratulate him.

Mr Chan takes a photo.

I've turned Berkhoff into a hero.

The minute I get out of the water I'm trapped by an angry mob.

'What's your game, Rude? You leading us on?'

'Yeah, dogbreath!'

'Get rid of Berkhoff or die, Rude.'

I'm in shock. Time's running out, and all I've done is jam the flying fox and make Berkhoff look like a hero. Maybe I *am* cursed. Maybe there is a Thing.

As we queue for afternoon tea, I mention this to Andy. He shrugs and takes some biscuits. He says the water may have been blocking my pheromones but we can't worry about that now. We have to focus on the bivouac in the mountains.

The bivouac is probably our last chance to set up humiliating experiences. Most of tomorrow morning is taken up with talks about the wildlife and nature features of the area, and tomorrow afternoon we go home. As we eat, we work out that we have only fourteen hours, including night-time, to do the job. We go over things we can do.

It would be good to make Berkhoff so furious that he does that silly skip. One obvious way of making him furious would be to put something in his sleeping bag to give him a scare. Another good way would be to hide something horrible in his food and only tell him when he's swallowed it. We feel we're starting to get somewhere. The trouble is, we'll have to play it by ear.

Our discussions are interrupted by Mr Chan banging a tin cup on his table for silence and handing out question sheets to complete on the bivouac. Then Berkhoff bangs *his* cup for silence and gives another lecture on safety and sticking with the group.

The man who runs the place reminds us to watch out for snakes, which in this area are often deadly. Ms Pewty blows her whistle and says she's the person allocating tents. The only good thing at the moment is that she and Berkhoff are making a point of sitting as far away from each other as possible.

We collect all the gear and set off, slogging up the hill. Just as we get started discussing more options for Berkhoff, we're interrupted by a pine cone pegged at my head. It's Clint and Cunningham. They want to know what we've got planned. Since we've got nothing properly planned, I try to put them off. They insist with threats of violence, so I tell them the sleeping bag idea. Cunningham interrupts with a yell. He rummages around in his pockets and, weirdly, asks whether I want a bit of chocolate. The last thing I want is a fluff-covered bit of chocolate from the depths of Cunningham's shorts. But it's not advisable to refuse.

Faking enthusiasm, I go, 'Oh, thanks.'
He goes, 'Hold out your hand.'
He drops a dead snake into it.

Chapter 24

I hate to admit it, but it's perfect. It's only a small snake, but after all the talk about deadly snakes it will spin Berkhoff out totally. Clint and Cunningham are really taken with the idea. In fact, they want to be the ones who do it. I'm very tempted, but this is too important to wreck. I say they can help, but Andy and I will do the actual thing.

I must be mad.

We work out a plan.

As soon as we stop for the bivouac, Andy and I will put up our tent, then slip up the hill to where Berkhoff and Chan are pitching theirs. When we're sure they've finished, I will signal to Clint, who will cause a distraction while I take the snake from Andy, slip in the tent and stick it in Berkhoff's sleeping bag. This meets with general approval, and, in less than sixty seconds everyone apart from Caroline Dillinger and her gang is informed and anxiously awaiting the action.

We arrive. Andy and I pitch our tent and sneak up to hide. We crouch down, watching Berkhoff and Chan pitching their tents.

Mr Chan does his quickly, but Berkhoff's hopeless. Mr Chan helps him. The suspense is terrible. After what seems like ages, they look as if they've finished. I whistle down to Clint, who gives me a thumbs-up and whacks Cunningham's foot with a tent mallet. This causes a great distraction because Cunningham didn't know Clint was going to whack him with a tent mallet. He shouts, swears—and starts trying to beat Clint to a pulp. Berkhoff and Mr Chan go flying down the hill to split them up.

I turn to Andy. 'Quick, the snake!'

Andy says, 'No. I'm putting it in.'

'Andy, give it to me.'

'Rack off.'

This happens. You think you know someone and they go stupid on you. I could thump him but we don't have time.

I check no one's watching us, then unzip the tent. My heart is pounding crazily. My ears are all hot. We scramble in. Inside, the light's orange and everything is strangely quiet.

A green sleeping bag is laid out neatly. It's one of those posh, tight-fitting models with a hood that they use on expeditions up Mount Everest. It must be a pretty tight fit for someone as big as Berkhoff. I get this mental picture of him inside it. He looks like a big green caterpillar with a human head. I suddenly notice Andy. He's only reading a book he's found by the pillow . . .

I hiss, 'Andy. Give us the snake!'

'See this? It's about how to build your own CD player and tape deck.'

'For God's sake! The snake!'

Andy says, 'I'll do it.'

Before I can stop him, he throws himself across the top of Berkhoff's sleeping bag and stuffs the snake inside. But because the sleeping bag's such a weird body shape, he can't get the snake down to the feet part. He starts fumbling at the zip.

I hiss, 'Don't unzip it! Just lift the bag and shake it down.'

'I've done it now.'

'Well zip it up and let's get out of here.'

But he's not zipping the bag up at all. He's fumbling with something in the corner of the tent. He turns round, snorting with laughter—and holds up Berkhoff's enormous sandals. They are huge—in fact, they're like two great big flat fish—and normally I'd be laughing as well. But now I'm terrified.

'Do up the zip, Andy!'

Andy gives a big, snorty laugh, says, 'Bassett hound!' and hangs one sandal over each ear. I leap at the sleeping bag zip and start tugging it. Andy fights me to get it. He's still wearing Berkhoff's sandals on his head. We wrestle. Andy's laughing. I can't believe this psycho.

'Get lost, Andy!'

I yank. The zip whizzes up and stops. Andy's sock is stuck in it. I could cry.

'You bloody idiot!'

'Well, you did it.'

I tug at the zip.

'You'll have to take off your sock.'

This means taking off his running shoe. Unfortunately, it's tied in about fifteen different bows and knots. He struggles with them.

'What are all those knots?'

'It's what commandos do to keep their boots on in a crisis.'

I grab his foot and start yanking desperately at his shoe. I jump up to get a better grip, pulling Andy's leg up in the air with me. He yells with surprise. I could kill him. His leg is straight up in the air and the sleeping bag's dangling from his sock. I'm tugging frantically. Every time I yank, Andy bounces on his bum and yells. Berkhoff's sandals are still dangling from his ears. My heart is pounding.

His shoe comes off and I rip off his sock. He bursts out laughing.

'Stop laughing!'

'You're tickling my feet.'

Suddenly I hear Berkhoff's voice. He's talking to Chan.

'Quick! We'll have to leave the sock.'

'These are my best socks.'

'Andy, he'll kill us.'

I bundle him out. We dive into the bushes seconds before Berkhoff and Mr Chan arrive. We've left the tent door unzipped but they don't seem to notice.

As soon as they're inside their tents we rush down the hill into ours. Clint comes bursting in to find out what happened. We tell him. Cunningham's with Ms Pewty getting his foot bandaged.

I let fly at Andy. He's unconcerned. That makes me even angrier. I refuse to talk to him, which means not only that I don't get any help with the question sheet, but that we can't plan anything more together about Berkhoff.

The suspense grows as the evening wears on. We eat a horrible dinner of gluey pasta prepared by Team A. Ms Pewty hands out another worksheet. It's headed 'Know the Forest' and has line drawings of objects you're likely to find. There's a picture of a dried-up berry thing, with the words: 'What does this remind you of?' Clint writes, 'Me Grannees face.' Then there's singing round the campfire and a talent contest. Ms Pewty produces a guitar and sings tuneless folk songs about people going on strike. Berkhoff's watching her, looking alternately wistful and annoyed. Everyone's whispering and giggling. People start saying how tired they are and asking if they can go to bed.

Finally, it's time. We all go into our tents and watch until the teachers go up to theirs. Then everybody's outside, watching Berkhoff's tent. He's put the light on, so you can see his silhouette. Everyone gets the giggles because he's so huge. Ms Pewty comes out without her glasses and tells us all to go back to bed. As soon as she's gone, we're all outside again. Nobody is getting changed into pyjamas in case they miss anything. Berkhoff's getting into the sleeping bag ... Then Caroline Dillinger appears.

She's just got out the words, 'Ian Rude, have you put a dead snake ...?' when there's a terrible Tyrannosaurus bellow from up the hill. The orange tent is writhing like it's alive. Then, with a huge roar, Berkhoff comes storming out of the tent.

What have I done? My heart sinks.

Berkhoff comes thundering down the hillside, bellowing. I've never seen him so mad. He's wearing his big padded ski-jacket over his pyjamas. His feet are slapping wildly against the enormous sandals.

He roars, 'Who was it? Who was it? I'll teach you to play me up!'

Caroline Dillinger goes, 'Oh, Mr Berkhoff, it was Ian Rude, Mr Berkhoff!'

But I'm gone. I'm flying off down the hillside.

Berkhoff's yelling, 'I hit my head on the tent pole!'

I'm going like the wind.

'I split the bloody sleeping bag!'

I'm crashing through undergrowth, my heart pounding. Twigs are slashing my face. I don't know where I'm going, but I've got to get away from Berkhoff. I've certainly made him look stupid, but I'm not going to let him murder me. I can hear him calling me to come back. Other teachers are calling as well. Now the land is going upwards. I run up a hill and hide, panting, behind a big rock. The teachers are calling in the distance. No way I'm coming out yet. I wait until it's completely quiet, then I come out.

I head back towards the camp. With a bit of luck I can slip in without anybody seeing. By morning Berkhoff will have calmed down. I keep walking. And walking. I look at my watch. It's 2 a.m. I keep walking.

At two-fifteen, I realise.

I am completely lost.

Chapter 25

I shiver. The best thing is to stay where I am until they find me. I sit on a rock and look around. There's a bit of moonlight, but not much. There's a scuffling in the bush, but I can't see anything. I hear a low throaty growl. It's spooky. It makes me think of The Thing, but I push the thought aside.

Actually, I can't push the thought aside. Perhaps this is The Thing's way of finally making contact. The scuffling gets closer. My stomach turns with fear. There's another growl, and some spitting. Suddenly, there's a deafening yowl right next to my ear. I leap to my feet and run.

I run and run. I can't see where I'm going, but it doesn't matter. I smash through undergrowth. I jump over logs.

Everywhere I go there's yowling and spitting. I speed to the top of a huge rocky outcrop. I collide with something. It's The Thing. It's Berkhoff.

We both go, 'Aaah!'

I trip over something. It's his foot. He yelps. He's hopping about in his big sandals, swearing. A stone falls over the edge and I can hear it hitting branches and rocks as it falls. It seems to be falling for ever. We must be really high up. Berkhoff slips and grabs me. I slip. Suddenly, we're both clinging together on the edge, tottering and yelling.

'You stupid idiot!'

'Aaah!'

'You bloody fool, Rude!'

At that exact moment, there's a blood-curdling screech, and some horrible big animal drops out of a tree right on Berkhoff's head. It's biting and spitting and yowling. Berkhoff's bellowing and trying to push it off at the same time as hanging on to me.

He slips, and the three of us go screaming over the edge.

Woomp. I land on top of Berkhoff, then go rolling off and come to a halt next to a log. I struggle to my feet, panting and trembling with shock. Everything's quiet. The creature has gone. About five metres away I can see Berkhoff flat on his back.

I call out, 'Mr Berkhoff?'

Silence. My stomach does a somersault. I walk a few steps closer.

I squeak, 'Mr Berkhoff?'

Oh God, I've killed him. I hear a faint groan. He's alive! I hurry over. He's flat on his back.

'Mr Berkhoff? Are you okay?'

He's struggling to shift himself sideways. I can barely hear him whispering, 'Underneath ... under ... something ...'

I realise he's landed on something and wants to move. I try shoving him, but he's so heavy it's impossible. Finally, he takes a deep breath, groans and shifts his great rear end sideways. We peer through the moonlight to see what it is. It's about fifty centimetres long and dark-coloured. It's no rock, and it's definitely not a plant. It's a feral cat.

Squashed dead.

A laugh spurts out of me. I gulp it back. This is not funny. Except it is! Berkhoff landed on a cat and killed it! Poor cat, what a way to go, crushed by Berkhoff's enormous bum. At least death would have been instant. Another laugh spurts out of me. I can't help it. I think I'm getting hysterical.

Berkhoff's gasping ferociously, 'Very funny ... Mr Class Clown ... if you ever ... tell anyone ...'

He stops, and there's silence. My laughter turns instantly to panic.

'Mr Berkhoff?'

I hear a faint, breathless whisper. 'When it's light ... get help.'

'Yes, sir. Can I do anything for you, sir?'

A long silence. Then, almost inaudibly, 'No ...'

I'm alone. In a vast national park. With a dying man.

I become aware that I'm kneeling in a very uncomfortable position. I sit on the ground. I can't just sit here! I feel myself starting to cry. I try not to, in case it upsets Berkhoff, but I can't help it. I think of all those stories of people dying alone in the bush. I think of Mum and Dad, who at this moment are probably fighting and packing their bags. I think of Andy being so stupid in the tent and how I thought he was my friend but he's not, he's just some whacko nerd you can't rely on.

201

Despite everything I can't stop myself dozing. I curl up on the ground. I keep dreaming I'm falling. I'm cold. Sometimes Berkhoff groans. It's horrible, but not as horrible as when I think he's stopped breathing. I dream I'm back at school playing basketball. It turns into the shop, with me making Petrol Heads. I open my eyes and it's dawn.

I stand up, I've got it planned. I'll break twigs on bushes as I go to make a trail. I'll head downwards because Beringa, where the cabins are, is down the hill. Berkhoff has his eyes closed and his mouth open. I'm about to talk to him when I have a flash of fear. What if he's dead? I steel myself to call out to him. My voice comes out all husky and weird.

'Mr Berkhoff?'

His eyes flick open. He's staring at me without saying anything. It's horrible. It's as if he's looking right through my body and out the other side. I feel like running for my life, but I force a smile.

'See you, sir, I'll get help.'

He just looks at me. I know he's going to die. I walk away at a carefully slow pace so he won't think I'm rattled. I can feel his eyes staring into my back. I snap a twig to start the trail, and realise I'm deliberately taking my time because I'm scared to leave. I feel hollow. I feel like the last person on earth. Tears come into my eyes. I swallow them and set off.

I keep heading downwards. I find a creek and follow it, like you read the explorers did. I walk for what seems like forever through dense rainforest. The light is green. I keep breaking twigs for the trail. My hands get blistered because the twigs are bendy and won't snap, so I end up having to tear them. I'm starving. I find a bit of stale vegeburger sandwich in my pocket and eat it. I try not to think that Berkhoff might be dead. The sun gets higher, but it's cold. It clouds over. I hear a helicopter overhead but the vegetation above me is so thick I can't see it. I shout and wave but it flies on. I keep going.

The rainforest starts to thin out. Suddenly I'm in broad daylight and ahead of me the creek is disappearing over the edge of a cliff. I go carefully to the edge. Hundreds of metres below is a river, probably the river that feeds into the lake at Beringa. There's no way I can get down a cliff as steep as that. I'll have to go back.

I want to cry, but I tell myself to get a

grip. I sit for a moment, then turn and head back. I find a fork in the creek and follow that. I keep going until I see broken twigs on bushes and realise that I've walked in a big circle. Then I do cry. I flop down and sob. I feel better, and head on. I decide to sing to keep up my spirits. The first thing that comes to mind is one of Syd's country and western songs called 'I'll Be There', so I sing that.

When I get sick of it I count my steps and give up at a thousand and sixty. I sing 'I'll Be There' again. But it makes me feel choked because it's all about a man telling his little kid he'll always be there for him in spirit, even if he's physically gone. While I've never thought about the words before, it's occurred to me that maybe *my* Dad won't be there for me any more, except in spirit. In fact, he might already have left.

That's if I ever get home at all.

I get angry with myself. I tell myself to stop being a wuss. I have to get home to fix things up between my parents. I chuck a stone. I swear. I pick up a fallen branch and snap it to get my anger out. I stride on. Then I hear something. It's a faint buzzing in the distance. I head towards it.

It's chainsaws, which must mean loggers! I sob and start to run. Now I can hear lots of chainsaws. The forest opens out magically into grasslands. I run. I come out onto rolling hills of grass as far as the eye can see. The chainsaws sound closer, but where are the loggers?

The chainsaws rev, splutter and change gear. Am I hearing things? Then I see them, not loggers with chainsaws, but a line of trailbikes forty or fifty wide appearing over the crest of a distant hill. It's the Cannibals.

And right in the middle is Dad.

Chapter 26

I yell. I wave. I jump up and punch the air.
I'm crying my eyes out but I don't care.
Dad hugs me like there's no tomorrow. I
tell them about Berkhoff. I sob it's all my
fault, and I didn't mean to kill him. I say
how Berkhoff was attacked by the feral
cat and how he broke my fall. I don't
mention Berkhoff squashing the cat to
death because I'm ashamed I laughed
when Berkhoff was dying. I'm sobbing so
hard that it takes me a while to understand what Dad's saying. He's saying Berkhoff is alive. He's got a broken leg,
broken ribs and a punctured lung, but he's
going to be okay.

I want to ask Dad how things are
between him and Mum, but at that
moment a TV news team arrives by heli-

copter and a journalist is asking me questions. Then Dad and I get taken off to hospital in a rescue helicopter full of police.

Mum is at the hospital when I arrive. She hugs me and cries. I can't work out what's going on between her and Dad because they're both so concerned about me. I do notice, though, that they're being extremely nice to each other. Sort of, oddly nice. A lot of sugary smiles and nods. Mum's also being nice to the Cannibals, who've come to see me.

I wish I could speak to Mum and Dad to find out whether these sugary smiles are something sinister, but there's no chance. Either there are Cannibals present, or nurses. Then Terry arrives with Troy and an army of Pockys, who are all convinced the feral cat that attacked Berkhoff and me was the Big Tabby. Mum and Dad leave at the same time as the Pockys. Mum leans over, kisses me, and whispers, 'Get some sleep now, darling. Dad and I have some important news to tell you tomorrow.'

My heart grabs with fear. But she's gone.

I have dinner. I try not to brood. I'm

in a ward all on my own, so there's nobody to talk to. I notice a TV, and switch it on. I'm channel-surfing when I see my own face. I'm crying. I'm saying Berkhoff saved my life and he's the best teacher in school. My mouth drops open. I didn't say that! The newsreader announces that in one day, Berkhoff saved three students from drowning and another from being ripped apart by feral cats.

He is, she says, a national hero.

At which point, a mob bursts into the ward, led by Clint and Cunningham.

'Rude, you dumb dork!'

'They're giving Berkhoff a medal.'

'They reckon Berkhoff's being made Principal!'

It's a complete disaster—particularly because everyone in the school apart from Andy thinks I did it on purpose.

I try explaining reasonably. They drown me out. I try shouting. Clint screws up my mum and dad's Get Well card and throws it at me. Cunningham says I should go up to intensive care where Berkhoff is and pull out his plug.

Apparently everything at school is in chaos while the staff cash in on the only bit of good publicity the school has ever had. Mrs Mitchell is planning for the school choir and the Year 7 recorder band to perform on a rota for visiting TV news teams. Mr Thompson is writing a special song for Berkhoff's 'welcome back' concert. Three rooms on the second floor of the science wing are going to be called the Michael Berkhoff mathematics area. Mr Cobbett is coming back early from sick leave, and there's to be a new annual award called the Berkhoff prize for civic responsibility.

It's lucky I'm in hospital because I figure I'm soon going to be in need of serious medical care. In fact, Clint is just suggesting that the mob should grab hold of my hospital bed and push it at high speed down the nearest flight of stairs, when a whistle blasts. It's Ms Pewty. She blinks behind her glasses, frowns, sucks air through her teeth, and says, 'All right, everyone, move along, there's nothing here to see.'

Miraculously, they all file out apart from Andy. Cunningham shakes his fist. Ms Pewty hands me a box of chocolates, sits down, frowns anxiously and says, 'Now Ian, are you sure you're all right?'

I smile. She starts talking. But I'm not

listening. My mind is taken up with Berkhoff.

I suddenly register she's saying something important to Andy. It's about Africa.

Africa?

I say, 'I'm sorry, Ms Pewty. What did you say about Africa?'

She blinks, frowns and says, 'Are you sure you haven't got concussion, Ian? I've been talking to Andy about Africa for ten minutes. I'm going to live there.'

She explains that now Cobbett is back, the school doesn't need her. She's leaving for Melbourne tonight. 'Yes, I'm going to Africa as a volunteer aid worker at the end of the month. I've been planning it for a long while. I like to be of assistance, you see. And now that there's nothing to keep me here . . .'

She stops, blushing. I realise she's thinking about Berkhoff, who, of course, we said was married. I feel guilty. She's a really nice person. Much too nice for Berkhoff, of course, but then, I suppose, that was her affair.

She smiles, frowns, sucks air between her teeth, and gets up. 'Well, boys, this is goodbye. Ian, have a good think about joining the football team, and in moments of stress, remember to flex.'

She shakes hands and leaves. We watch her go.

Andy says, 'You realise Berkhoff'll be ten times worse without her?'

It's horrible to imagine. I remember I'm supposed to be angry with Andy, but, given the rest of my problems, I can't be bothered.

I say, absently, 'Yeah, he really liked her.'

I get an image of Berkhoff trying to impress Ms Pewty in the Principal's office. I remember his big meaty face beaming at her in Assembly.

I say, 'No doubt about it, Berkhoff would have followed Ms Pewty anywhere. Even Africa!'

There's a moment of silence while it sinks in. Andy looks at me.

I look at Andy.

Chapter 27

I leap out of bed. We run off up the corridor. No Ms Pewty. The lift's taken. We run down two flights of stairs to see if we can catch it. The doors open. No Ms Pewty. Gone. The last chance of getting rid of Berkhoff—gone.

'Ian, what on earth are you doing out of bed?'

It's her. I could kiss her cross-trainers.

I say, 'Ms Pewty, I . . .'

I realise I'll have to tell her we deliberately wrecked her relationship. For the first time it strikes me what a terrible thing that was to do. I should confess, but I'm too ashamed.

I splutter, 'You have to see Mr Berkhoff.'

'Mr Berkhoff? Why?'

She's blushing and annoyed.

I go, 'He ... well ... he ...'

Andy butts in, 'He said he had to talk to you.'

'About what?'

Andy says, 'I don't know. But it seemed really important. He said he had to speak to you personally, Ms Pewty. He was very insistent.'

It's lucky that Andy is such a star student because teachers tend to believe him. Ms Pewty hesitates. You can see she's wondering whether Berkhoff deserves her time after all he's done to her. She frowns, sucks air in through her teeth and looks at her watch. I hold my breath. Will she buy it?

She says, 'Let's go.'

We set off for Intensive Care. I'm in a panic. We'll have to tell them the truth. How else can we patch things up between them, let alone get him to go to Africa with her? I whisper this to Andy. He disagrees. He says it's too late for the truth. If we confess now, they'll realise students have been messing in their affairs. They'll both be totally humiliated. They might even try to save face by pretending they never cared about each other. She'll go to Africa and he'll let her.

I whisper, 'So what do we do?'

Andy shrugs and whispers, 'Let them talk it through.'

That sounds reasonable—until we get to Intensive Care. We find Berkhoff unconscious with tubes coming out all over him and a thing like a vacuum cleaner hose down his throat which, the nurse explains, means he can't talk.

Ms Pewty turns to us angrily.

'What's going on here? He can't even talk and you boys said he'd asked for me.'

We just stand there. Then Andy stammers, 'He did, Ms Pewty, it's just he ... wrote a note.'

We're getting in deeper.

I cut in, 'Yes, Ms Pewty. He wrote your name on a piece of paper, but his hand was shaking so much that only Andy and me understood.'

She's looking at me dubiously. I start to gabble.

'In fact, he had to write it three times before we worked out what he was trying to tell us. He really wants to talk to you, Ms Pewty. He's desperate.'

'Did he really?'

I'm taken aback because her voice is all soft. At that moment Berkhoff opens his eyes and sees Ms Pewty, who frowns, smiles, sucks air between her teeth and whispers gently, 'Mr Berkhoff? Do you need a pen?'

Berkhoff blinks. You can see he's thinking that's a strange question to ask someone in his position. He blinks again, to check he's not dreaming.

At which point, Ms Pewty gets all excited.

'Ian, look! He's trying to blink the message! Is that right, Mr Berkhoff? Are you trying to tell me something? Ian says you have a message for me. Blink once for yes and twice for no.'

Berkhoff blinks three times in total confusion.

Ms Pewty's confused. She turns to me. 'Three blinks? What does three mean?'

Andy says, 'Maybe it's "don't know". Like in "yes", "no", and "don't know". Or maybe it's, "That's for me to know and you to find out".'

Berkhoff's eyes roll furiously. He glares at me and blinks. Then he stares back at Ms Pewty, blinks three times, turns to me and blinks twice. This is terrible! I was so worried about how to get them together, I hadn't thought what would happen when they did. I know I have to butt in before things get any worse, but I don't know what to say.

I play for time. I blurt out, 'Ms Pewty, three blinks means ... it means ...'

This is stupid. I have to confess.

I blurt, 'This is enough, Ms Pewty. I have to tell you.'

She says, 'Tell me what, Ian?'

'To tell you ... tell you ...'

Andy's signalling for me to shut up. Ms Pewty is staring, eager-eyed, expecting some vital message from Berkhoff. Berkhoff is frowning like he wants to murder me. I'm dying. I know the minute I tell the truth Ms Pewty will hate me, Berkhoff will vow eternal vengeance, Andy will call me a dobber, and my life will be made so miserable I won't have time to help my parents.

Then a miracle happens. Because I know how to do it. It's a huge risk, but what have I got to lose?

I take a deep breath, turn to Ms Pewty and say, 'Ms Pewty, Mr Berkhoff wants me to tell you what he said about you on the mountain. When he was unconscious—I mean delirious, delirious with pain, Ms Pewty—so he probably won't remember.'

Ms Pewty's rapt with attention. Berkhoff's eyebrows have joined together in bewilderment.

'He made me promise that if he was dead or sick I would tell you all the following things. So I will.'

I gulp. I look at Ms Pewty, lick my dry lips and say, 'He said he dreamed of a life in Africa. With you, Ms Pewty.'

Ms Pewty gasps. Berkhoff's eyebrows shoot upwards.

I say, 'He said he wished you weren't married, because, since he's unmarried himself, he gets really lonely ...'

Ms Pewty bursts in, 'But I'm not married!' She leans over to him. 'I thought you were! Who told you I was married?'

I carry on hurriedly, 'Stuck on that freezing cold mountain yesterday, Ms Pewty. In agony. Nearly dying ... He said ...'

I've gone blank. *What can Berkhoff have said?*

'He said ...'

Oh no, what? What can he have said? Ms Pewty's staring at me absolutely rapt. Andy looks terrified. Berkhoff's eyes are fixed open in amazement.

'He said, "Yesterday ... all my ... troubles ... seemed ... so far away ..." '

Oh no! That's the Beatles!

I'm hoping it will pass unnoticed, but Ms Pewty gasps and says, all choked-up, 'But those are the words of "Yesterday".'

'Exactly, Miss! And that's why Mr Berkhoff started singing it!'

'He sang? With a punctured lung!'

Oops.

'Not very well, Ms Pewty. But with lots of expression.'

Will she swallow it? Will he? I glance from one to the other. Andy is baring his teeth with suspense. Then Ms Pewty turns to Berkhoff, sucks air through her teeth and smiles. She's all dewy-eyed behind her glasses. He's blinking madly. She takes Berkhoff's big meaty hand. Still staring at him, she smiles, sucks some more air, and softly sings, 'Yesterday ... all my troubles seemed so far away ...'

Berkhoff's eyes are fixed on her. He puts his other hand on hers and squeezes it. She gives a little sob. Suddenly, she starts to belt the song out at the top of her voice. Some old guy in the corner starts yelling. Nurses rush over.

Andy drags me out, and we collapse,

exhausted, on a bench. We discuss the chances of Berkhoff going. They're good. Berkhoff would be mad to give up any woman who liked him, let alone someone as nice as Ms Pewty. In any event, there's nothing more I can do. My big problem now is my parents. Andy wishes me luck. I'll need it.

Chapter 28

When I get back to my ward I find Mum waiting to see me, but she's got Granny Pocky with her so I can't bring up anything personal. I sleep badly.

Next morning, Dad arrives to take me home. My plan is to ask him as soon as the nurse leaves us alone, but she doesn't. She even insists on taking me down to the hospital entrance in a wheelchair. When we get there, who should be sitting in the lobby but Syd and Skull, who've come with Dad for the ride.

We arrive at our place. We say goodbye to Syd and Skull. We walk into the empty kitchen. My heart is pounding.

I turn to Dad, and say, 'Dad, I ...'

At which point, Mum, Mick, Terry, Granny Pocky and Troy all jump out from the storeroom to give me a welcome home party. Syd and Skull return.

The party seems to go on for ever. We have gallons of tea and a cake in the shape of a feral cat. I try to interpret what's happening between Mum and Dad. They're still being super-nice to each other. Dad gets Mum a chair. She smiles at him, then at me, then back at him again. They whisper. I remember an article I once read at the dentist. It said people at the end of a relationship often put on a big act for their children.

Now Mum's making a fuss of Troy. He starts screaming because he wants my bit of cake. I give it to him.

He says, 'Nick off!'

One by one, people leave. Now it's just Mum, Dad and me. My mouth is dry. My heart starts pounding. Mum and Dad start doing the sugary smiles and awkward whispering.

Attempting to sound casual, I say, 'So. What's this big news you're planning to tell me?'

There's a silence. Mum gives me a desperate little smile and looks at Dad anxiously.

'Steve? Shall I tell him or will you?'

'Oh, you, I think.'

Mum doesn't know where to start.

She smiles and says gently, 'This is going to come as a shock, Ian, and you'll take a while to adjust, but ...'

Get on with it!

She beams. 'I'm pregnant!'

They both laugh, hug me, laugh some more, ask what names I like, show me my old baby clothes, make cups of tea, laugh ...

I'm stunned. I finally interrupt all the gooing and say, as calmly as I can, 'Look, I ... When I left for camp I thought ... I thought you were breaking up.'

They're both amazed.

Dad says, 'But why?'

This is bizarre.

'Weren't you fighting about the Cannibals coming to the shop? And Dad being a Cannibal?'

Mum smiles at me, then at Dad. She says, 'Oh, well, I must admit I was a bit worried about all that, but then the Cannibals were all so concerned and helpful when you went missing. Then they rescued you and I thought to myself that really, I couldn't want better friends and customers than these people, and a better partner

222

than your dad, even if his bike-riding worries me. And there you are.'

And there you are. Just like that. I'm astonished. I keep asking them questions and reminding them of the way they were fighting. They're mystified I should have taken it so seriously. Some bits they don't even remember. In fact, they're so happy and soppy and obsessed with dragging out old baby photos of me with a bare bum that I feel like telling them to shut up and act their age. And then I realise how stupid that is of me. One thing this whole business has taught me is that, however frustrating Mum and Dad are, I care about them, and I'd be totally miserable if they split. And actually, it might be quite fun being someone's big brother.

I give up and join in the general celebrations. I don't think I'll ever understand their relationship. As Andy says, every marriage is a mystery.

Talking of mysterious marriages, Ms Pewty put off leaving Yarradindi, and shortly afterwards she and Mr Berkhoff announced their engagement. Then, before the two of them left for overseas, they came back for a farewell assembly. Berkhoff was led to a special seat on stage with Mr Cobbett. Members of the student representative council helped various old people to stagger into places behind him. We sang the school song. Clint Pocky and Cunningham did arm-farts in the chorus.

Cobbett gave a speech. Berkhoff gave a speech. Ms Pewty gave a speech. Cobbett gave another speech, and presented Berkhoff with an atlas, and Ms Pewty with a polished wooden box containing a set of that bowling game, boules. She said she'd always wanted a set of boules, which caused a tidal wave of hysterics until Mrs Mitchell got menacing. Members of the student representative council gave Berkhoff and Ms Pewty a video made by the Year 11 media studies class two years ago to celebrate the school's fiftieth birthday. The school captains gave all the guests flowers.

Then, as the finale, the school band and choir launched into Mr Thompson's 'welcome back' song for Mr Berkhoff, with the words 'farewell to' substituted for 'welcome back'. Lauren Tate accidentally tipped the sidedrum onto Caroline Dillinger's foot, so they had to start again.

And that was it. Berkhoff was gone.

As for my powers, they've never come back. I don't know whether it was all coincidence, or whether they were caused by my pheromones or what. Were they supernatural? Again, I don't know.

But here's the weirdest thing. Even though I know I no longer have any powers, and maybe never did, the entire school, apart from Andy, is still convinced that I do. I'll always be the kid who got rid of Berkhoff, the maths teacher from hell. What's more, the rumour is I did it by turning up the power on his ventilator until he promised faithfully to go.

As far as Teenage Energy Pills are concerned, it's the same sort of thing. Nothing you can say can ever make people believe they are not powerful potions. They point to the fact that the Year 10 cricket team won its first match in living memory after taking Teenage Energy Pills. They go on about Cunningham losing six kilos, and how the acne of the Ratbag Criminal Element disappeared practically overnight. They don't make the connection with the fresh fruit, vegetables and gallons of water Mum told them to take. Or, for that matter, the placebo effect.

As Andy says, never underestimate the power of the human mind.

Personally, I've given up arguing. I go along with it. And, if Dad happens to over-order lentils, or our soy milk is about to go off, or Mick's mung beans are rotting in their plastic bags, I just tell people that we have a new consignment of really powerful health foods, and put the lot on special. The queues go all around the block. We're famous for miles.

Andy's cow stomach only came third in the Young Scientist competition, and Syd and Terry's entry for the funniest home video didn't come anywhere at all. But all three of them persist. Syd and Terry are working on a video about Syd setting his trousers alight. Andy is being mysterious in our kitchen with tweezers, potato peelings and an electric fan.

As for Dad's Harley, he has it on permanent loan from Syd in return for doing all Syd's accountancy work. In fact, Dad now does accountancy work for all the bikers in the area. He's got a little office at the back of El Gringo, which Mum and Dad have taken over and called (under Dad's influence) El Rude Gringo. Mum's only condition of keeping Wozza as manager was that, for health reasons, he should shave.

My sister Daisy was born three weeks early, after an emergency dash to hospital with an escort of Cannibals. She is incredibly cute. She thinks I'm wonderful, and the only thing I require of her is that she never learns to say 'Nick off.'

And I mustn't forget the vegeburger. It's become quite famous. After people found out it was all I had to eat on the mountain, they started buying it to take camping. We now sell heaps in the shop, plus a few boxes to shops around the country. It's not the burger empire that Dad imagines it is, but, doing our arithmetic, it's not bad.

Which brings me to our new maths teacher. She's called Mrs Martinez-Wong and she's tiny. She has green and blue hair, a chain linking her nostril with her left ear, and big boots. She doesn't need a Castle.

Boy, does she not need a Castle.

So that's that! I'm still short, but I can handle it. Occasionally, I dream about being stuck with Berkhoff on the mountain. And, at school, Andy and I sometimes laugh about him bellowing, 'I'll teach you to play me up,' doing a Tyrannosaurus roar and skipping savagely along between the desks. Mostly, I don't think about him at all.

But the other day . . .

Okay, let me explain. It's a Wednesday evening. I've finished all my homework. I've washed up with Mick, who's been staying with us since last month when his mudbrick hut partially dissolved in the floods. I've played with Daisy, I've put out the shop's scraps for Ripper and I'm settling down with Dad to watch the big game. The news is on, but I'm hardly watching because I'm arranging my popcorn and two cans of Coke for easy access.

I'm vaguely aware that the TV screen is showing a reporter standing outside a small group of buildings in the middle of a vast dry plain. He's talking seriously about sanctions or drought—the usual news report sort of thing.

Then, something, I don't quite know what, draws my attention to the screen. Now, I should tell you that Dad says I'm imagining it. He was watching the news as well, and he says he saw no such thing. But I know his mind was taken up with the do-it-yourself commercial he and Syd and the Cannibals are planning for the vegeburger. And I know what I saw.

As the reporter is talking there's some kind of commotion going on in the distance. There's shouting and crashing. Then, from one of the buildings right in the corner of the picture, bursts a bunch of kids. They're yelling and looking over their shoulders. They go pelting across the grasslands for dear life. Is it a lion? A rogue elephant? It's clearly none of these things. Those kids are laughing.

I crouch down in front of the screen. I try to block out what the reporter is saying. I concentrate hard on the background and the little building from where the children came. And what I see, bursting out from the building, is a blob. It's shouting and wearing khaki shorts and scattering chickens. My mouth drops open. It can't be . . .

But there's a Tyrannosaurus roar, a voice bellows, 'I'll teach you to play me up!'

And, I swear, skipping furiously across the African plains, goes Mr Berkhoff . . .

Linda Aronson
Kelp

Seaweed. It's green. It stinks. And 14-year-old
Emily Tate feels like she's sinking in it.

Emily wants to be the world's youngest self-
made multi-millionaire. Instead, she's stuck on
a tiny slimy island with her eccentric family
and their belching smelly seaweed factory for
company.

Her only ray of hope is a young hunk with a
mobile phone and pots of cash. Trouble is,
she hasn't met one . . . yet.

A selected list of titles available from Macmillan and Pan Books

The prices shown below are correct at the time of going to press. However, Macmillan Publishers reserve the right to show new retail prices on covers which may differ from those previously advertised.

LINDA ARONSON
Kelp	0 330 36949 0	£3.99

TIM WINTON
Lockie Leonard, Human Torpedo	0 330 34067 0	£3.99
Lockie Leonard, Scumbuster	0 330 34068 9	£3.99
Lockie Leonard, Legend	0 330 35496 5	£3.99

MORRIS GLEITZMAN
Blabber Mouth	0 330 33283 X	£3.99
Sticky Beak	0 330 33681 9	£3.99
Belly Flop	0 330 34522 2	£3.99
Water Wings	0 330 35014 5	£3.99

All Macmillan titles can be ordered at your local bookshop
or are available by post from:

Book Service by Post
PO Box 29, Douglas, Isle of Man IM99 1BQ

Credit cards accepted. For details:
Telephone: 01624 675137
Fax: 01624 670923
E-mail: bookshop@enterprise.net

Free postage and packing in the UK.
Overseas customers: add £1 per book (paperback)
and £3 per book (hardback)